Legal Disclaimer

This is a work of fiction. Names, characters, organizations, places, events, and incidents are either the product of the author's imagination or used fictitiously. Any resemblance to actual persons, living or dead, or actual events is purely coincidental.

The author does not intend to portray or suggest any real-world criminal activity, law enforcement conduct, or political corruption depicted herein as factual. This work is intended solely for entertainment purposes and should not be construed as an accurate representation of real-world events, individuals, or institutions.

Dedication

To those who stand against the tide of corruption, their resolve unbroken in the face of shadow and ruin.

Prologue

The rain hammered down like a judgment from above, each drop a cold, accusing finger tapping on the conscience of those who dared to tread these streets. In the heart of the city's forgotten underbelly, where the neon lights flickered weakly against the encroaching darkness, a lone figure stood in the mouth of a narrow alley, their breath misting in the frigid air. The figure clutched a small, sleek device in their trembling hand, its surface slick with rain and sweat, its encrypted contents a Pandora's box of secrets that could unravel the very fabric of power in this crumbling metropolis.

A second shadow emerged from the gloom, their silhouette sharp and menacing, the collar of their coat turned up against the relentless downpour. The exchange was swift, almost silent a murmured word, a nod, and the device changed hands, disappearing into the folds of the second figure's coat. The air between them crackled with unspoken threats and promises, the weight of the transaction hanging heavy in the damp night. As the second figure turned to leave, their footsteps echoing off the wet pavement, the first figure remained rooted to the spot, eyes wide with a mix of fear and resignation, knowing that the web of corruption they had just fed would only grow tighter, more suffocating.

In this city, where justice was a commodity traded in back alleys and whispered deals, the device was more than a tool it was a key to a labyrinth of lies, a map to the rot that festered beneath the surface. And somewhere in the shadows, Jonah Raines, a man who still believed in the thin blue line, would soon find himself ensnared in its perilous threads.

Chapter 1: The Discovery

The rain came down in relentless sheets, a cold shroud over the city that blurred the line between night and despair. Jonah Raines sat in the passenger seat of the unmarked sedan, his broad shoulders hunched against the damp chill seeping through the cracked window. The wipers slapped a steady rhythm against the windshield, fighting a losing battle against the deluge, while the glow of a streetlamp painted streaks of yellow across his weathered face. At forty-six, Jonah carried the weight of twenty years on the force lines etched deep around his gray-blue eyes, a jaw clenched tight with the stubborn resolve that had kept him going when others had burned out. His dark hair, streaked with silver, clung to his forehead beneath the hood of his coat, and his hands rested heavy on his knees, calloused fingers twitching with restless energy.

Beside him, Sarah Lin gripped the steering wheel, her slim frame taut with focus. She was younger thirty-four, with a decade less wear on her soul her short black hair plastered to her head from an earlier dash through the storm. Her dark eyes flicked between the rearview mirror and the tenement across the street, where a flickering neon sign buzzed faintly over Slim Thompson's known haunt. Sarah was cautious where Jonah was relentless, her steady presence a counterweight to his bulldog tenacity. They'd been partners for three years, long enough to trust each other implicitly, their dynamic forged in late-night stakeouts and bloody crime scenes.

"Think he's in there?" Sarah asked, her voice low, cutting through the drumming rain.

Jonah grunted, peering through the water-streaked glass at the crumbling building. "He's got nowhere else to go. Slim's a creature of habit deals out of that dump like it's his office."

The apartment block loomed like a decayed tooth in the city's rotting jawline, its brick facade tagged with graffiti that bled into the shadows gang signs, prayers, curses scrawled in desperation. The streets around it were a labyrinth of despair, lined with pawn shops and liquor stores, their neon signs casting a sickly glow over puddles that reflected the hopelessness of the place. This was the city Jonah had sworn to protect, a metropolis teetering on the edge of collapse, its soul sold off piece by piece to corruption and greed. He believed in the badge, clung to it like a lifeline, but nights like this made that faith feel like a fraying thread.

Sarah shifted in her seat, adjusting her grip on the wheel. "You look like hell, Jonah. When's the last time you slept?"

He smirked, a dry twist of his lips that didn't reach his eyes. "Sleep's overrated. Keeps me sharp."

"Liar." She shot him a sidelong glance, her tone softening. "You're running on fumes. This job's gonna kill you if you don't ease up."

"Been trying for twenty years. Hasn't managed it yet." He rubbed a hand over his stubbled jaw, the rasp of skin on bristles loud in the cramped car. "What about you? Still think you can save this place?"

Sarah's gaze drifted to the tenement, her expression tightening. "Someone's got to try. Otherwise, what's the point?"

Jonah didn't answer, letting the silence stretch between them. She still had that spark, that faint flicker of optimism he'd lost somewhere along the line maybe after his divorce, or the first time he'd watched a kid bleed out in an alley, or the hundredth time he'd seen a case buried under red tape. Sarah reminded him of who he'd been once, before the city ground him down to raw edges and stubborn grit.

"Alright," he said finally, nodding toward the building. "Let's move. He's not gonna arrest himself."

They stepped into the rain, the cold biting through their coats as they crossed the street, boots splashing through oily puddles. Jonah's hand rested on the butt of his service pistol, a familiar weight at his hip, while Sarah flanked him, her own weapon drawn and held low. The tenement's front door hung crooked on its hinges, and they slipped inside, the air hitting them like a punch mildew and rot, thick enough to taste.

The hallway was a dim tunnel of peeling wallpaper and broken lightbulbs, the floor littered with trash discarded needles, crumpled cans, a child's shoe lying forlornly in the corner. Jonah's boots crunched on glass as he led the way to apartment 3B, his breath fogging in the damp chill. Sarah stayed close, her steps silent, her eyes scanning the shadows for threats.

At the door, Jonah raised a fist and pounded twice, the sound echoing like a gunshot. "Police! Open up, Slim!"

Silence, then a scuffle footsteps, a crash. Jonah met Sarah's gaze, a wordless signal passing between them, and they kicked the door in unison. The cheap wood splintered inward, revealing a squalid living room sagging couch, overturned table, the air thick with the sour tang of unwashed bodies and stale smoke. Slim Thompson bolted from the bedroom, a wiry blur in a stained hoodie, his sneakers skidding as he vaulted the couch and crashed through the back window onto the fire escape.

"Damn it!" Jonah lunged after him, his heavier frame slower but relentless, while Sarah shouted, "He's running!"

The fire escape groaned under Jonah's weight, rusted metal slick with rain as he descended, gripping the railing to keep from slipping. Slim hit the alley below, his silhouette darting toward the street, and Jonah followed, landing hard on the wet pavement. The chase was on, his boots pounding through puddles that splashed up his legs, the city a blur of neon and shadow around him. Slim was fast, desperation lending him wings, but Jonah was a bloodhound, driven by a stubborn refusal to let another crook slip away.

The alley twisted past overflowing dumpsters and graffiti-smeared walls, the air sharp with the stench of garbage and gasoline. Slim glanced back, his eyes wide with panic, and stumbled over a pile of discarded crates. Jonah closed the gap, tackling him to the ground in a tangle of limbs and curses, the impact jarring his knees against the asphalt. Slim thrashed, bony elbows flailing, but Jonah pinned him with a knee to his back, yanking the cuffs from his belt.

"Stay down, you little bastard," Jonah growled, snapping the cuffs tight.

Sarah caught up, her gun trained on Slim, her chest heaving. "Nice tackle. You good?"

"Yeah," Jonah panted, hauling himself up, rain streaming down his face. "Let's see what he's got."

He patted Slim down, hands moving with practiced efficiency. Plastic baggies of pills meth, probably tumbled out, along with a wad of crumpled bills. Then his fingers brushed something else: a small, sleek device, its dark screen glinting faintly in the dim light. It wasn't a burner phone or a cheap tracker; its design was too refined, too high-tech for a lowlife like Slim. Jonah turned it over in his hand, frowning, a prickle of unease creeping up his spine.

"What's this?" he asked, holding it up.

Slim smirked, blood trickling from a split lip. "You'll never figure it out, pig. Bigger than you."

Jonah locked eyes with him, searching that defiant glare. There was fear there, buried deep, a flicker that didn't match Slim's usual bravado. He pocketed the device, the weight of it heavy against his thigh, and hauled Slim to his feet. Sarah holstered her weapon, her brow creasing as she glanced at the spot where the device had disappeared.

"Think it's something?" she asked quietly.

"Don't know," Jonah muttered. "But it's not his usual junk."

They marched Slim to the squad car, the rain soaking through their clothes, the dealer's sneakers dragging in sullen defiance. The drive to the precinct was a tense blur, the hum of the engine drowned out by Jonah's racing thoughts. That device it didn't fit. Slim was small-time, a bottom-feeder in the city's criminal ecosystem. What was he doing with something that looked like it belonged in a tech lab?

The precinct was a fortress of peeling paint and flickering lights, its air thick with the bitter scent of burnt coffee and sweat. Jonah handed the device to the tech team three overworked geeks hunched over outdated computers while Sarah processed Slim's booking. Captain Marcus Hale approached, his heavy tread announcing him like thunder. Hale was a broad-shouldered bulldog of a man, his gray hair buzzed short, his face a roadmap of hard years and harder choices. He'd been Jonah's rock for a decade, a steady hand in a sea of chaos, but tonight his expression was guarded.

"Good bust," Hale said, his voice a low rumble. "What's with the gadget?"

"Found it on Slim," Jonah replied, crossing his arms. "Looks encrypted. Could be a lead."

Hale's eyes flicked to the tech desk, then back to Jonah, a shadow crossing his features. "Probably just burner tech. Don't waste your time focus on the report."

Jonah bristled, the dismissal hitting him like a slap. "Captain, this isn't standard gear. My gut says it's big."

"Your gut's been wrong before." Hale's tone was flat, almost too casual. "Leave it to the techs. That's an order."

Jonah nodded stiffly, but the words gnawed at him. Hale wasn't usually this quick to brush him off something was off-kilter, a subtle shift that set his instincts buzzing. He filed the report, his pen scratching across the page, but his mind was elsewhere, circling back to that sleek little device. When the tech team logged it into evidence, Jonah lingered, watching as they bagged it and turned away. On impulse, he retrieved it from the locker, slipping it back into his pocket, protocol be damned. If Hale wouldn't listen, he'd figure it out himself.

Home was a sparse apartment on the city's edge, a bachelor's pad of worn furniture and unwashed dishes. The rain tapped against the window like impatient fingers as Jonah sank into his chair, the device in hand. The place was quiet too quiet save for the hum of his ancient laptop booting up. Eight years divorced, no kids, no life beyond the job; this was his refuge, or his prison, depending on the night. Tonight, it felt like both.

He shouldn't do this. Taking evidence home was a line he rarely crossed, a breach of the rules he'd built his career on. But that knot in his gut wouldn't loosen, and Hale's evasiveness had lit a fire under it. Jonah plugged the device into his laptop, his fingers steady despite the tremor of doubt in his chest. He'd seen too much crooked cops, buried cases, a city eating itself alive and this felt like the tip of something uglier.

The screen flickered, a wall of code greeting him, and Jonah's lips pressed into a thin line. Encrypted, alright military-grade, maybe. He thought of Slim's smirk, that flicker of fear, and the pieces didn't fit. Not yet. He leaned back, staring at the device, the weight of his decision settling over him like a shroud. Whatever this was, it was his now his burden, his fight. The city's shadows stretched long and deep, and Jonah Raines was about to step into them alone.

Chapter 2: Into the Shadows

Jonah Raines sat hunched over his laptop in the dim glow of his sparse apartment, the only light coming from the screen and a flickering streetlamp outside. The rain had stopped, leaving the city cloaked in a damp, oppressive silence, broken only by the occasional drip from the leaky faucet in the kitchen. His fingers hovered over the keyboard, trembling slightly not from the cold, but from the weight of what he was about to do. The sleek, encrypted device he'd taken from Slim Thompson lay connected to his laptop, its dark surface reflecting the pale blue of the screen. Jonah's breath came in shallow bursts as he stared at the wall of code before him, the encryption a fortress he was determined to breach.

He shouldn't be doing this. Taking evidence home was a violation, a crack in the code he'd sworn to uphold. But Captain Hale's dismissal had been too quick, too casual, and Jonah's gut honed by twenty years on the force screamed that something was wrong. Slim was a bottom-feeder, a small-time dealer who peddled cheap highs to the desperate, not the kind of crook who carried military-grade tech. Whatever this device held, it was bigger than Slim, bigger than the precinct, and Jonah wasn't about to let it slip through his fingers.

He launched the decryption software a relic from a past case, acquired from a hacker who'd owed him a favor. The program whirred to life, lines of code scrolling across the screen as it chewed through the encryption layer by layer. Jonah leaned back in his chair, rubbing his temples, the faint hum of the laptop filling the room. His apartment was a testament to his life's narrow focus: a sagging couch, a coffee table scarred with cigarette burns, a kitchenette cluttered with takeout containers. No photos, no mementos just the bare essentials of a man who'd given everything to the job and had little left to show for it.

Minutes stretched into hours, the night deepening around him. Jonah's eyes burned from staring at the screen, but he didn't blink, didn't move, his entire being fixated on the progress bar inching toward completion. Finally, with a soft chime, the software cracked the last barrier, and the screen flooded with data rows upon rows of names, dates, transactions. Jonah's heart slammed against his ribs as he scrolled through the list, his breath catching in his throat.

It was a ledger, meticulous and damning. Bribes, payoffs, illegal deals a roadmap to the city's corruption laid bare. Politicians, CEOs, high-ranking cops all implicated in a web of graft that stretched from the precinct to city hall and beyond. Jonah's hands shook as he recognized names: Councilman Edward Greer, a polished reformer with ambitions for the mayor's office; Victor Kane, a businessman whose name whispered through the city's elite like a ghost; and then, like a punch to the gut, Officer Mike Daniels.

Mike. His friend, his mentor, the man who'd pulled him out of a burning car after a chase gone wrong, who'd stood by him through the divorce, who'd shared beers and war stories after tough shifts. Mike's name was there, stark and undeniable, linked to a series of payments labeled "cleanup" and "silence." Jonah's stomach twisted, a wave of nausea rising in his throat. He scrolled further, each name a fresh betrayal: Deputy Chief Alvarez, second-in-command of the entire force, a man who'd built his career on iron-fisted justice; Captain Marcus Hale, his own superior, the rock he'd leaned on for a decade.

Jonah slammed the laptop shut, his breath ragged, the room

spinning around him. He staggered to the kitchen, splashing cold water on his face, but the shock lingered, a cold fist clenched around his heart. How deep did this go? How many people he'd trusted, respected, were part of this machine? The system he'd bled for, the badge he'd worn like a shield it was all a lie, a house of cards built on blood and greed.

He needed to tell someone, needed to share the weight of this before it crushed him. Sarah. She was the only one he could trust, the only one who hadn't been tainted by the city's rot. He grabbed his burner phone a relic from an undercover op and dialed her number, his fingers trembling.

"Jonah?" Sarah's voice was groggy, thick with sleep. "It's two in the morning. What's wrong?"

"I need to see you," he said, his voice tight, barely controlled. "Now. Meet me at the diner on 12th. It's important."

A pause, then, "Alright. Give me twenty minutes."

He hung up, grabbed his coat, and slipped out into the night, the ledger's data burned into his mind like a brand.

The diner was a 24-hour refuge on the city's outskirts, its neon sign buzzing faintly against the dark. Inside, the air was thick with the smell of burnt coffee and grease, the booths worn and sticky. Jonah sat in the corner, nursing a cup of sludge that passed for coffee, his laptop open on the table. The place was nearly empty a lone trucker at the counter, a waitress wiping tables with mechanical boredom. Sarah slid into the booth across from him, her face pale under the harsh fluorescent lights, her eyes searching his.

"What is it, Jonah?" she asked, her voice low, tense.

He turned the laptop toward her, the ledger's glow casting shadows across her face. "Look."

She scrolled through the list, her breath hitching as she recognized the names. "Jonah, this is… this is insane. Mike?

Alvarez? The captain?"

"It's real," he said, his tone flat, final. "I decoded it myself. This isn't some hoax it's a goddamn roadmap to hell."

Sarah's hands trembled as she pushed the laptop back. "We need to take this to someone. Internal Affairs, the feds someone who can handle it."

Jonah shook his head, his jaw tight. "If Alvarez is dirty, IA's probably compromised too. And Hale he told me to drop it, Sarah. He knew something."

Her eyes widened, a flicker of fear crossing her face. "You think the captain's involved?"

"I don't know what to think anymore." Jonah rubbed his eyes, exhaustion and anger warring inside him. "But I can't trust anyone in the precinct. Not until I know who's clean."

Sarah leaned forward, her voice dropping to a whisper. "So what do we do?"

Jonah stared at the screen, the names burning into his memory. "We dig deeper. Find out how far this goes, who's pulling the strings. But we can't do it from inside the system not if they're watching."

She reached across the table, her hand closing over his. "Jonah, this could get you killed."

"I know," he said, meeting her gaze. "But if we let this slide, the city's finished. Someone has to stop it."

Sarah hesitated, then nodded, her loyalty overriding her fear. "Alright. What's the plan?"

Before Jonah could answer, a shadow fell across the table. He looked up to see a man in a long coat standing at the diner's entrance, his eyes scanning the room with cold precision. Something about him the way he moved, the bulge under his coat set Jonah's nerves on edge. Then, two more men entered, their gazes locking onto Jonah and Sarah with predatory intent.

"Shit," Jonah muttered, his hand drifting to his holster. "We've got company."

Sarah's eyes widened as she followed his gaze. "Who are they?"

"Doesn't matter. We need to leave. Now."

They slid out of the booth, Jonah tossing a crumpled twenty on the table as they headed for the back exit. The men moved to intercept, their hands slipping inside their coats. Jonah's heart pounded, adrenaline flooding his veins. He shoved Sarah toward the kitchen door, his voice low and urgent. "Go! I'll cover you."

She hesitated, but he pushed her forward. "Move!"

The kitchen was a blur of steam and clattering pans, the air thick with the smell of frying oil. Jonah drew his pistol, his back to the wall as he peered around the corner. The men were closing in, their weapons now visible silenced pistols, professional gear. These weren't street thugs; they were hitters, sent to silence him.

A gunshot cracked, the bullet burying itself in the wall beside Jonah's head. He returned fire, the muzzle flash lighting up the dim corridor, and one of the men grunted, stumbling back. Sarah kicked open the back door, and they spilled into the alley, the cold air hitting them like a slap.

"Run!" Jonah shouted, grabbing her arm as they sprinted down the narrow passage, their boots splashing through puddles. Behind them, the remaining men gave chase, their footsteps pounding like war drums.

The alley twisted past overflowing dumpsters and rusted fire escapes, the city a maze of shadows and dead ends. Jonah's lungs burned, his legs heavy with fatigue, but he pushed on, dragging Sarah with him. They rounded a corner, nearly colliding with a chain-link fence that blocked their path.

"Climb!" he barked, boosting her up. She scrambled over, dropping to the other side, and Jonah followed, his coat snagging on the wire. Another gunshot rang out, the bullet pinging off the metal inches from his hand.

They hit the ground running, cutting through a parking lot and onto a deserted street lined with shuttered storefronts. The men were still behind them, relentless, their silhouettes dark against the neon haze. Jonah spotted a subway entrance ahead, its gate ajar, and made a split-second decision.

"This way!" he yelled, pulling Sarah toward the stairs. They plunged into the tunnel, the air thick with the smell of damp concrete and decay. The darkness swallowed them, the only light a faint glow from the platform below.

Jonah led the way, his boots splashing through puddles, the echoes of their pursuers fading but not gone. They reached the platform, empty and silent, the tracks stretching into the void. He pulled Sarah behind a pillar, his breath ragged, his gun still clenched in his hand.

"Listen," he whispered, his voice barely audible over the drip of water. "You need to get out of here. Go to a friend's place, somewhere safe. Lay low until I contact you."

Sarah's eyes were wide, her face pale in the dim light. "What about you? Where are you going?"

"I don't know yet," he admitted, his mind racing. "But I can't go back to my apartment they'll be watching it. I need to disappear, figure out my next move."

She grabbed his arm, her grip fierce. "Jonah, don't do this alone. We can fight this together."

He shook his head, gently prying her fingers loose. "You've got a life, Sarah. A kid. I won't drag you down with me."

Tears welled in her eyes, but she blinked them back, nodding. "Just... don't get yourself killed, okay?"

"I'll try," he said, managing a faint smile. "Now go. Before they find us."

She hesitated, then turned and ran toward the exit, her footsteps echoing in the tunnel. Jonah watched her go, a pang of guilt twisting in his chest. He'd brought her into this mess, and now he was cutting her loose. But it was the only way to keep her safe.

He waited until she was out of sight, then slipped deeper into the subway, blending into the shadows. The city above was a jungle, its predators circling, but Jonah was a survivor. He'd find a way to expose the truth, even if it meant tearing down everything he'd once believed in.

The safehouse was a crumbling tenement on the city's edge, its windows boarded up, its halls reeking of mildew and neglect. Jonah had used it before, during undercover ops, a bolt-hole known only to a few. He slipped inside, the door creaking on rusted hinges, and made his way to the basement, where a cot and a battered desk awaited.

He set up his laptop, the ledger's data glowing in the dark. His apartment was compromised, his life as a cop over. He was a ghost now, a rogue operative with nothing left to lose. But he had the ledger, and with it, a chance to bring the whole rotten system crashing down.

Jonah's fingers flew over the keys, digging deeper into the files, tracing the web of corruption. Names, dates, amounts it was all there, a blueprint for dismantling the city's elite. But he needed more than data; he needed leverage, proof that couldn't be ignored or buried.

His thoughts drifted to Elena Morales, a journalist who'd been sniffing around police corruption for years. She was ambitious, relentless, and hungry for a story that could make her career. If he could get the ledger to her, she might be able to blow it wide open.

But trust was a luxury he couldn't afford. Elena was a wildcard, her motives as murky as the city's underbelly. Still, she was his best shot at getting the truth out.

He grabbed his burner phone and dialed her number, his voice low and urgent. "Elena, it's Jonah Raines. I've got something you'll want to see."

A beat of silence, then, "Detective Raines. This is unexpected. What kind of something?"

"The kind that could take down half the city," he said. "But it's dangerous. You in?"

Another pause, then, "Where do we meet?"

Jonah smiled grimly. The game was on.

The city stretched out below the safehouse window, a sprawl of lights flickering like dying stars. Jonah stood there for a long moment, the weight of the ledger pressing against his chest. He'd spent his life chasing justice, believing in the thin blue line that held the chaos at bay. Now, that line was gone, erased by the very people he'd sworn to stand beside.

He thought of Mike Daniels, the memory of their last beer together sharp and bitter. It had been after a bust, a rare victory against the city's endless tide of crime. Mike had clapped him on the shoulder, grinning through the exhaustion, and said, "We're the good guys, Jonah. Don't ever forget that." The words echoed now, hollow and mocking, as Jonah replayed them against the ledger's cold evidence.

He sat back down at the desk, the laptop's hum a steady companion in the silence. The data was overwhelming hundreds of entries, each one a thread in the tapestry of corruption. He filtered the list, searching for patterns, connections that might lead him to the puppet masters. Mike's name appeared again and again, tied to operations Jonah had worked on, cases he'd thought were clean. The betrayal cut deeper with every line, a knife twisting in his gut.

Deputy Chief Alvarez's entries were more cryptic, coded references to "meetings" and "adjustments." Jonah cross-referenced dates, his mind racing as he pieced together a timeline. Alvarez had been at the precinct the day Slim was brought in, his presence a shadow over the interrogation. Had he known about the device? Had he ordered Hale to bury it?

Jonah's fingers paused over the keys, his breath catching as he found an entry dated three months back a payment to Hale labeled "Thompson disposal." Slim's arrest hadn't been random; it was a cleanup, a loose end tied off by the very people Jonah had trusted to uphold the law.

He leaned back, the chair creaking under his weight, and stared at the ceiling. The apartment's damp chill seeped into his bones, but he barely noticed. His world had shifted, the ground beneath him crumbling away. He was alone now, a man without a badge, without a home, without a side to fight for. But he wasn't done not yet.

The burner phone buzzed on the desk, snapping him out of his reverie. It was Sarah. He hesitated, then answered, his voice rough. "You okay?"

"Yeah," she said, her tone strained. "I'm at my sister's place. What about you?"

"Safe, for now," he lied, glancing at the boarded-up window. "Stay put, Sarah. Don't come looking for me."

"Jonah, I can help "

"No," he cut her off, sharper than he'd intended. "You've done enough. This is on me now."

A long silence stretched between them, heavy with unspoken words. Finally, she said, "Be careful, alright? I don't want to lose you."

"You won't," he said, though the promise felt empty. "I'll call when I can."

He hung up before she could argue, the phone cold in his hand. He couldn't drag her deeper into this not when he didn't know who was hunting him, or how far their reach extended. The attack at the diner had been too precise, too coordinated. Someone knew he had the ledger, and they'd stop at nothing to take it back.

Jonah returned to the laptop, his resolve hardening. He couldn't go back to his apartment not with it likely under surveillance but he needed supplies: cash, clothes, a weapon that wasn't tied to his badge. The safehouse had the basics, but he'd have to move soon, find a new hole to crawl into.

He pulled up a map of the city on his screen, plotting his next steps. Elena would meet him tomorrow, at a spot he'd chosen for its anonymity a derelict pier on the east side, far from prying eyes. If she was serious about the story, she'd bring resources, contacts he could use to amplify the ledger's impact. If she wasn't... well, he'd deal with that when it came.

For now, he needed rest, though sleep felt like a distant dream. He lay on the cot, the springs groaning under him, and stared at the cracked ceiling. The city hummed outside, a beast that never slept, its pulse a mix of desperation and defiance. Jonah closed his eyes, the ledger's names scrolling through his mind like a litany of the damned.

Morning came gray and heavy, the sky a slab of concrete pressing down on the city. Jonah woke stiff and sore, the cot doing little to ease the ache in his bones. He checked the laptop still powered, still secure and packed it into a battered duffel bag along with the burner phone and a spare clip for his pistol. The safehouse felt like a cage now, its walls closing in, and he knew he couldn't stay.

He slipped out the back, keeping to the alleys, his coat pulled tight against the damp. The streets were waking up, delivery trucks rumbling past, workers shuffling to their shifts. Jonah moved like a shadow, his eyes scanning for tails, his hand never far from his gun. The city was a predator, and he was prey now marked, hunted, alone.

The pier was an hour's walk, a stretch of rotting wood and rusted metal jutting into the river. Jonah arrived early, scoping the area for threats. It was deserted, the wind carrying the tang of salt and decay. He found a spot behind a stack of crates, out of sight but with a clear view of the approach, and settled in to wait.

Elena arrived on time, her figure cutting through the mist in a trench coat and boots. She was younger than he'd expected, mid-thirties, with sharp eyes and a guarded stance. She spotted him and approached, her movements cautious but deliberate.

"Raines," she said, her voice low, clipped. "You look like hell."

"Feel like it too," he replied, stepping out to meet her. "You bring what I asked?"

She held up a flash drive, dangling it between her fingers. "Encryption tools, untraceable. You've got something big, don't you?"

"Bigger than you can imagine." He pulled the laptop from his bag, powering it up. "Take a look."

She plugged in the drive, her eyes narrowing as the ledger loaded. She scrolled through it, her breath catching as she recognized the names. "Jesus. Daniels, Alvarez, Kane this is a powder keg."

"And it's already lit," Jonah said, his tone grim. "They came for me last night. Barely got out."

Elena's gaze flicked to him, assessing. "You're a dead man walking, you know that?"

"Been that way for years," he said, a bitter edge to his voice. "Question is, can you do something with this?"

She nodded, her jaw tight. "I've got contacts editors, whistleblowers. If this checks out, I can get it front-page. But I need time, and you need to stay alive long enough to back it up."

"Working on it," he said, shutting the laptop. "Copy what you need. I'm not sticking around."

She worked quickly, transferring the files, her fingers flying over the keys. "Where are you going?"

"Somewhere they won't find me," he said, though he hadn't figured that part out yet. "I'll reach out when I've got more."

Elena handed the laptop back, her expression hard. "Don't die on me, Raines. This story's no good without a source."

He gave her a faint nod, then turned and walked away, the pier creaking under his boots. The city loomed ahead, a labyrinth of danger and secrets, but Jonah was in too deep to turn back. He'd abandoned his old life, shed it like a skin that no longer fit. Now, he was something else a rogue, a ghost, a man with nothing left but the truth and the will to see it through.

The rest of the day passed in a blur of movement and shadow. Jonah found a flop house on the west side, a cash-only dive where questions weren't asked. He paid for a week upfront, locking himself in a room that smelled of stale smoke and despair. The ledger stayed with him, a constant companion, its weight both burden and lifeline.

He spent hours poring over it, cross-referencing names and dates, building a picture of the corruption's scope. It wasn't just payoffs there were hits, cover-ups, entire operations run off the books. Mike's name tied to a warehouse raid Jonah remembered, one where evidence had mysteriously vanished. Alvarez linked to a string of "accidents" that silenced potential leaks. Kane's entries were the most chilling tersely worded orders for eliminations, delivered through proxies like a king commanding his knights.

Jonah's mind churned, piecing it together. This wasn't a loose network; it was a machine, oiled with money and blood, its gears turning at the highest levels. He was a cog that had slipped free, and now the machine wanted him crushed.

Night fell, the room's single bulb casting harsh shadows. Jonah sat on the edge of the bed, his pistol in his lap, the laptop glowing beside him. He couldn't stay here long every hour increased the risk of being found. But he couldn't run blind either. He needed a plan, a way to strike back before they closed the net.

His thoughts drifted to Sarah, safe for now, he hoped. He'd pushed her away, but the ache of it lingered, a reminder of what he'd lost. The precinct, his badge, his friends all gone, replaced by this solitary war. Yet he couldn't stop, not when the ledger held the key to tearing it all down.

He powered down the laptop, stashing it under the mattress, and lay back, the gun still in his hand. Sleep came fitfully, broken by dreams of gunfire and betrayal, the city's dark heart pulsing through his veins. Tomorrow, he'd move again, find a new shadow to hide in. Tomorrow, he'd take the fight to them.

For now, he was Jonah Raines, rogue cop, keeper of secrets, a man on the edge of oblivion and he wasn't going down without a fight.

Chapter 3: The Factory

The industrial district sprawled like a festering wound across the city's northern edge, a tangle of rusted steel and crumbling concrete that hadn't seen prosperity in decades. Jonah Raines crouched behind a splintered wooden pallet, his breath shallow, his eyes scanning the shadows. The air hung heavy with the tang of rust and oil, a bitter taste that clung to the back of his throat. Beside him, Elena Morales adjusted the straps of her backpack, her movements precise despite the tension etched into her face. The factory loomed ahead, its silhouette jagged against the bruised sky, a relic of a bygone era now repurposed for darker deeds.

Jonah shifted his weight, the gravel beneath his boots crunching faintly a sound too loud in the oppressive silence. He'd been a cop long enough to know that silence was a lie; it hid things, dangerous things. The duffel bag slung over his shoulder pressed against his ribs, its contents a high-sensitivity microphone, a digital recorder, and a spare clip for his pistol rattling softly as he moved. Elena glanced at him, her dark eyes catching the faint glow of a distant streetlamp, and gave a curt nod. She wasn't a cop, but she'd earned his trust over the past weeks, her journalist's instinct for the truth matching his own stubborn drive.

"Perimeter's thin," she whispered, her voice barely a breath. "Two at the front gate, one roving east. Loading dock's our best shot."

Jonah grunted in agreement, his mind already tracing the route they'd planned. They'd spent the previous day holed up in a dingy motel room, studying grainy surveillance photos and a faded blueprint Elena had pried from a reluctant source. The meeting was set for midnight Victor Kane's lieutenants gathering to carve up their empire's next moves. If they could capture Kane's voice on tape, ordering the elimination of witnesses like T.J. Jackson, they'd have the kind of evidence that could crack the conspiracy wide open. But it meant walking into the lion's den, and Jonah knew lions didn't sleep lightly.

"Stay tight," he said, his tone clipped. "We plant the gear, record the bastard, and ghost out. No detours."

Elena's lips twitched, not quite a smile. "No heroics, got it."

They moved as one, slipping along the edge of the compound, their shadows merging with the hulking shapes of abandoned machinery. The loading dock yawned open ahead, a black mouth framed by sagging doors, the interior a maze of crates and rusted conveyor belts. Jonah led the way, his pistol drawn, its weight a cold comfort in his hand. The air inside was thick, stagnant, laced with the metallic reek of old grease and the faint buzz of flickering fluorescents overhead. Each step echoed faintly, a reminder of how exposed they were.

The blueprint guided them through the labyrinthine corridors, past rows of silent machines that loomed like sentinels in the gloom. Jonah's pulse thudded in his ears, a steady rhythm that kept him grounded as they climbed a rickety metal staircase to the catwalk above the factory floor. The foreman's office sat at the far end, its grimy windows overlooking the cavernous space below a perfect perch for Kane's lieutenants to plot their next betrayal.

They settled into position behind a rusted girder, the catwalk creaking under their weight. Jonah unzipped the duffel, pulling out the mic a sleek, black device with a range that could pick up a whisper from fifty feet. He rigged it to the recorder, testing the levels with a flick of his thumb, while Elena kept watch, her binoculars pressed to her eyes. The office was still empty, its battered table and mismatched chairs bathed in the dim glow of a single bulb.

Minutes dragged into an hour, the silence stretching taut as a wire. Jonah's legs cramped, his knees aching against the cold metal, but he didn't move. Patience was a weapon he'd honed over years of stakeouts, though it never got easier. Elena shifted beside him, her breath hitching as headlights swept across the factory floor below. Engines growled, then cut off, replaced by the crunch of boots on gravel.

"Here we go," she murmured, lowering the binoculars.

Figures emerged from the shadows six men, their suits incongruous against the factory's decay, their faces hard and unreadable. They filed into the office, their voices a low rumble through the glass. Jonah adjusted the mic, angling it toward the window, his fingers steady despite the adrenaline spiking through him. Then, Victor Kane stepped inside, and the air seemed to tighten.

Kane was a predator in a tailored coat, his silver hair gleaming under the light, his movements deliberate, almost languid. He carried himself like a king, not a criminal, his icy gaze sweeping the room before he took his seat at the table's head. Jonah's jaw clenched, a familiar anger simmering beneath his skin. This was the man who'd turned the city into his personal fiefdom, who'd buried good cops and innocent lives under layers of corruption.

"Gentlemen," Kane began, his voice smooth as polished steel, "we've got loose ends to tie up. Messy ones."

The scarred lieutenant to his left leaned forward, his bulk straining his jacket. "Jackson?"

Kane nodded, a faint smile curling his lips. "T.J. Jackson's been talking. To cops, to reporters whoever'll listen. He's a liability we can't afford."

Jonah's gut twisted. T.J. was a lowlife, sure a hustler who'd traded secrets for leniency but he'd been desperate, not disloyal. Kane's casual dismissal of his life was a gut punch, a reminder of how little humanity remained in this game.

"Take him out," Kane continued, his tone flat. "Quietly. No traces."

Another lieutenant, a wiry man with a nervous tic, spoke up. "What about the others? The ledger's got names witnesses, informants."

"Eliminate them," Kane said, his eyes narrowing. "No witnesses, no links. We burn the past and move on."

The mic captured every word, its tiny red light blinking steadily as the recorder whirred. Jonah's mind raced, cataloging the implications how many lives hung on this order, how many families would fracture because of it. He glanced at Elena, her face pale but resolute, her fingers gripping the edge of the catwalk.

Then the office door swung open again, and a new figure stepped inside a woman, her posture rigid, her face half-hidden by the hood of a dark jacket. Jonah's breath caught as she turned, the light catching her features: Carla Ramirez, the rookie cop he'd leaned on for the factory tip. Her presence hit him like a freight train, confusion and dread crashing through him.

"Officer Ramirez," Kane said, his voice tinged with something almost warm. "You're late."

Carla's hands twitched at her sides, her voice unsteady. "Had to shake a tail. Sorry."

"Sit," Kane ordered, gesturing to a chair. "You've earned your place here."

Jonah's thoughts spiraled. Carla his source, his reluctant ally was sitting at Kane's table, not as a prisoner, but as a player. He'd assumed she was trapped, coerced by her brother's debts, but this looked different. Willing. Complicit. Betrayal clawed at him, sharp and bitter, though a part of him clung to doubt, searching her tense frame for signs of duress.

Elena's hand brushed his arm, urgent. "Jonah, we need to move."

He shook his head, his eyes locked on Carla. "Not yet. I need to know."

Kane leaned back, his fingers steepled. "Officer Ramirez has been our eyes inside the precinct. Shipments cleared, raids diverted she's kept us ahead of the game."

Carla stared at the table, her knuckles white. "I've done what you wanted. My brother "

"Is breathing because of you," Kane cut in, his tone hardening. "Keep it that way. Now, Raines. What's he got?"

Jonah's blood turned to ice. Carla's gaze dropped further, guilt radiating from her. "He's digging. Deep. The ledger, the shipments he's close."

"Then he's a problem," Kane said, his voice a blade. "End him."

The words landed like a blow, confirmation of what Jonah had feared: he was a target, marked by the machine he'd sworn to dismantle. Elena was already packing the gear, her movements swift and silent, but Jonah couldn't tear his eyes from Carla. Was she a pawn or a traitor? The answer mattered, but not now not when survival hung by a thread.

"We've got it," Elena hissed, shoving the recorder into her bag. "Let's go."

Jonah nodded, forcing his focus back to the present. They retraced their path, slipping through the shadows, the factory's weight pressing down like a living thing. But as they neared the loading dock, a shout shattered the silence a guard, his flashlight beam slicing through the dark, catching Elena's sleeve.

"Intruders!" the guard roared, his pistol barking a shot that sparked off a nearby beam.

Jonah yanked Elena behind a crate, his own gun up and

firing, the recoil jarring his arm. Bullets tore through the air, splintering wood and pinging off metal, the chaos erupting like a storm. More guards poured in, their shouts overlapping, their footsteps pounding closer.

"We're boxed in," Elena gasped, ducking as a round whizzed past her head.

Jonah scanned the dock, his mind racing. The exit was a gauntlet of gunfire, their position crumbling by the second. He squeezed off two more shots, dropping a guard, but the odds were stacking against them five, six men now, closing the net.

A sharp crack split the air, distinct from the guards' weapons, and one of them dropped, a clean hole in his forehead. Another crack, another body down. Jonah's head snapped up, spotting a figure on the catwalk a hooded silhouette, a sniper rifle braced against their shoulder, their shots precise, surgical.

"Who's that?" Elena breathed, her voice shaking.

"No clue," Jonah said, but gratitude flickered through him. The sniper's fire carved a path, scattering Kane's men, giving them a lifeline. "Move!"

They sprinted, weaving through the chaos, the sniper's rounds covering their flank. Bullets whined past, one grazing Jonah's arm, a hot sting he ignored. They burst through the dock doors, the night air slamming into them, cold and raw. The sniper's fire stopped, the figure melting into the shadows as abruptly as they'd appeared.

They didn't slow, pounding across the gravel to the sedan parked a block away. Jonah slid behind the wheel, the engine roaring to life, tires screeching as they peeled into the city's neon haze. His arm throbbed, blood seeping through his sleeve, but he gripped the wheel tighter, his mind churning.

"Carla," he muttered, the name a curse and a question.

Elena, panting beside him, clutched the recorder. "She's scared, Jonah. You saw her she's not all in."

"Doesn't change the facts," he snapped, his voice rough. "She's with them. And they want me dead."

"We've got Kane on tape," she said, holding up the device. "His voice, his orders it's enough to burn him."

Jonah glanced at her, the fire in her eyes cutting through his anger. "Can you get it out there? Make it stick?"

"I'll do more than that," she vowed. "I'll make sure no one can ignore it."

The city blurred past, a sprawl of light and shadow, but Jonah's thoughts stayed in the factory Carla's haunted face, the sniper's timely shots, Kane's cold decree. They'd escaped, but the war had escalated, the stakes climbing higher with every mile. The sniper Cipher, he'd learn later remained a ghost, their motives a riddle he couldn't solve yet.

For now, they had evidence, a weapon to wield. But the cost was steep, trust fracturing under the weight of betrayal and blood. As they vanished into the night, the factory's silhouette faded, but its echoes lingered, a promise of battles still to come.

Chapter 4: The Reckoning

The elevator hummed softly as it ascended, carrying Jonah, Sarah, and Cipher toward the penthouse and the reckoning that awaited them. The air inside the mirrored box hung heavy, thick with unspoken words and the faint tang of sweat. Jonah stood rigid, his knuckles white around the grip of his pistol, its cold steel a lifeline against the chaos brewing in his chest. Sarah shifted beside him, her breath uneven, fingers brushing the holster at her hip as her eyes flicked to the glowing numbers ticking upward. Cipher leaned against the back wall, hood low, a shadow among shadows, their silence louder than the hum of machinery.

Below them, the city sprawled in its filth a maze of flickering neon and broken promises. Kane's tower loomed above it all, a glass dagger thrust into the night sky, its penthouse a glittering perch for a man who thought himself untouchable. Jonah's jaw tightened. Weeks of chasing leads, dodging bullets, and sifting through the ledger's cryptic filth had led to this moment. Kane's reign ended tonight or they did.

The elevator dinged, a soft chime that felt like a gunshot in the stillness. The doors slid open, revealing a hallway of obscene luxury: plush crimson carpet, walls lined with paintings that screamed wealth, the air laced with the stale bite of cigar smoke. Jonah stepped out first, his boots sinking into the pile, every nerve on edge. Sarah followed, her pistol drawn low, her face a mask of focus frayed at the edges. Cipher brought up the rear, their rifle cradled like an extension of their body, their steps silent as a predator's.

They moved toward the double doors at the hall's end, their polished surfaces reflecting warped versions of themselves three figures on a collision course with fate. Jonah glanced at Sarah, her lips pressed thin, then at Cipher, who met his gaze with a nod sharp as a blade. No words. They didn't need them.

Jonah drove his boot into the doors, the wood cracking like thunder, splinters scattering across the marble beyond. They stormed in, weapons high, the room unfolding before them in a tableau of excess. Floor-to-ceiling windows framed the city's jagged skyline, lights twinkling like stars fallen to earth. Sleek leather furniture gleamed under a chandelier's cold glow, and a long glass table dominated the center, surrounded by Kane's inner circle six lieutenants in tailored suits, their faces hardening at the intrusion.

Victor Kane sat at the head, his silver hair catching the light, his hands steepled casually before him. Beside him loomed Overlord, a mountain of a man with a scarred cheek and eyes like chipped ice. The air stank of power, of money, of blood long since scrubbed clean.

"Hands up!" Jonah's voice cut through the room, raw and unyielding. "Nobody moves."

Sarah swept her pistol across the lieutenants, her stance steady despite the tremor in her breath. Cipher slid to the right, rifle trained on Overlord, the red dot of their laser sight dancing on his chest. The room froze, a tableau of tension stretched taut.

Kane didn't blink. He leaned back, a smile curling his lips slow, deliberate, venomous. "Jonah Raines. I'd say I'm surprised, but that would imply I didn't see this coming." His voice was silk over steel, every syllable dripping with control. "You've got guts, I'll give you that. Not much else, but guts."

Jonah's finger twitched on the trigger, his pulse hammering in his ears. "It's over, Kane. The ledger, the recordings we've got it all. You're done."

Kane's smile widened, his eyes glinting with something dark, something amused. "You think a few scraps of paper and some garbled audio will topple me? This city's mine, Raines. I built it. I own it. You're just a gnat buzzing around a lion."

Overlord shifted, his hand inching toward his belt, but Cipher's voice sliced through the air, low and lethal. "Try it. See how fast you bleed."

Kane raised a hand, stilling his enforcer, his gaze never leaving Jonah. "Let's not be hasty. I'm curious what exactly do you think you've won here? A moral victory? A clean conscience?" He laughed, a dry, cutting sound. "You're a fossil, Jonah. A man who thinks the world still bends to right and wrong. It doesn't. It bends to me."

Jonah's chest burned, his anger a live wire sparking beneath his ribs. "You've poisoned everything. The precinct, the courts, the people who trusted you. But we've got proof now. You can't bury this."

Kane's expression shifted, the amusement fading to something colder, sharper. "Proof? You mean the crumbs I let you find? You're a dog chasing its tail, Raines. And you've brought friends to the slaughter." He tilted his head, his voice dropping. "Didn't you ever wonder who fed you those leads?"

A shadow moved at the edge of the room, and Jonah's world tilted. Captain Marcus Hale stepped into the light, his gray hair tousled, his service pistol glinting in his hand. His face was lined with exhaustion, regret etched into every crease, but his stance was firm.

"Jonah," Hale said, his voice rough, pleading. "Drop it. Walk away."

The words hit like a fist, knocking the air from Jonah's lungs. "Hale?" His pistol wavered, disbelief clawing at him. "What the hell are you doing?"

Hale's eyes flickered, heavy with something Jonah couldn't name. "It's bigger than you know, son. Kane's not the head of this snake he's just the fangs. I've been keeping the peace, holding the line. You're tearing it all apart."

Jonah's hands shook, his grip tightening on the gun as betrayal sank its teeth in. Hale his mentor, his anchor through years of grime and disillusionment standing with Kane. "You sold us out. You sold *me* out."

Hale took a step forward, his gun steady, his voice cracking. "I protected you. Kept you clear of the worst of it. But you wouldn't stop digging. You forced my hand."

Sarah's whisper cut through the haze, soft and urgent. "Jonah…"

Kane leaned forward, his smile a blade. "Beautiful, isn't it? Your captain, your hero, groveling at my feet. Tell me, Raines how does it feel to be the last honest man in a city of liars?"

Jonah's vision swam, Hale's betrayal a wound deeper than any bullet. Fifteen years fifteen years of trust, of late-night coffee runs and hard-earned respect shattered in a heartbeat. "You were supposed to be better than this," he said, his voice breaking. "You taught me to fight for something."

Hale's shoulders sagged, a flicker of the old man Jonah knew surfacing in his eyes. "I did. But the fight's rigged, Jonah. Always has been. I'm sorry."

He raised his pistol, the barrel locking on Jonah's chest. The room shrank, time stretching thin, every sound amplified the click of Hale's safety, Sarah's sharp intake of breath, the thud of Jonah's own heartbeat. Then a gunshot split the silence, deafening and final.

Hale's eyes widened, a red flower blooming across his chest. He staggered, his gun slipping from his fingers, clattering to the marble as he crumpled, lifeless, at Kane's feet.

Sarah stood frozen, her pistol still raised, smoke curling from the barrel. Her face was a mask of horror, tears cutting tracks through the grime on her cheeks. "I he was going to " Her voice broke, a sob swallowing the rest.

Jonah stared at her, numb, the weight of her choice crashing over him. She'd killed Hale. For him. The man who'd trained them, who'd patched them up after bad calls, who'd been family gone in a flash of muzzle fire.

Kane's laughter shattered the moment, cold and jagged. "Oh, this is exquisite. The loyal little soldier turns executioner. You've got a flair for drama, Sarah."

Cipher's rifle snapped to Kane, their voice a hiss. "Shut your mouth."

Kane ignored them, his eyes locked on Jonah. "You see it now, don't you? The rot goes all the way down. Your friends, your allies they'll all turn on you in the end. Just like Hale."

Jonah's voice was steel, forged in grief and rage. "You don't get to talk about him. You made him this."

Kane shrugged, unfazed. "I didn't pull the trigger. She did." He nodded toward Sarah, who flinched as if struck. "And you you're the fool who dragged her into this mess. How many more will die for your crusade, Raines?"

"Enough," Cipher said, their finger tightening on the trigger. The shot was a crack of thunder, precise and brutal, punching through Kane's forehead. His head snapped back, blood spraying across the glass table, his body slumping forward in a heap of silk and ruin.

The room exploded. Lieutenants lunged for weapons, chairs toppling, shouts ringing out. Jonah moved on instinct, diving behind a sofa as bullets tore through the air, shredding leather and splintering wood. Sarah dropped beside him, her pistol barking as she took down a man reaching for a shotgun. Cipher flowed through the chaos, their rifle a metronome of death each shot a kill, each movement deliberate.

Jonah's ears rang, the world a blur of muzzle flashes and shattered glass. He leaned out, firing at a lieutenant scrambling for the panic room, the man's scream cut short as he fell. Overlord roared, charging through the fray, his bulk smashing a table aside. Jonah met him head-on, slamming his pistol into the man's jaw, the impact jolting his arm. Overlord snarled, blood dripping from his mouth, and swung a fist that caught Jonah's shoulder, sending him staggering.

Pain flared, but Jonah ducked the next blow, driving his elbow into Overlord's gut. The big man grunted, doubling over, and Jonah finished it with a knee to the face, cartilage crunching as Overlord hit the floor, out cold.

Silence fell, heavy and abrupt, the air thick with gunpowder and the coppery scent of blood. Jonah stood panting, his ribs aching, his hands slick with sweat. Sarah rose beside him, her face ashen, her gun trembling in her grip. Cipher stood over Kane's body, their hood still shadowing their eyes, the rifle now slung across their back.

"We're done here," Cipher said, their voice flat, clinical. "Move."

Jonah nodded, his throat raw. He spared one last look at Hale sprawled on the marble, blood pooling beneath him, his face frozen in a mask of regret. A wave of nausea hit, but Jonah swallowed it down. No time. Not now.

They slipped into the service corridors, the penthouse's sterile luxury giving way to concrete and flickering fluorescents. The stairwell echoed with their descent, boots pounding, breaths ragged. Fifty floors felt like fifty miles, the weight of what they'd done pressing harder with each step.

At the bottom, an alley waited dark, damp, the air sharp with the bite of exhaust. A black SUV idled in the shadows, its engine a low growl. Cipher slid behind the wheel, Jonah and Sarah piling into the back, the doors slamming shut as they peeled out into the night.

Jonah slumped against the seat, the city blurring past the window neon streaks and looming towers, indifferent to the blood they'd spilled. Sarah's hand found his, her fingers cold and trembling, her voice a whisper. "We got him, Jonah. It's over."

He turned to her, her tear-streaked face lit by passing lights, and saw the lie in her words. Kane was dead, but the ledger's secrets stretched further, a web of corruption still choking the city. Hale was gone, a piece of Jonah torn out and left bleeding on that penthouse floor. And Sarah she'd crossed a line tonight, one that would haunt her as long as she lived.

Cipher's eyes met his in the rearview mirror, sharp and unyielding. "This isn't the end. Kane was a head, not the body."

Jonah nodded, the truth settling like ash in his lungs. "I know."

The SUV cut through the streets, the city a beast stirring in its sleep, its hunger undimmed. They'd won a battle, carved a wound into its hide, but the war loomed larger than ever. And as the adrenaline ebbed, leaving only exhaustion and loss, Jonah felt the weight of it all the cost of their reckoning, and the price still to come.

The penthouse faded into memory, but its ghosts clung tight. Jonah's mind replayed the night in fragments: the splintered doors, Kane's smug grin, Hale's final, broken apology. Sarah's gunshot echoed loudest, a sound he'd never unhear. She sat silent beside him now, staring at her hands as if they belonged to someone else, the blood invisible but indelible.

They'd planned this for days weeks, if you counted the sleepless nights poring over the ledger, tracing Kane's empire through coded accounts and whispered names. Cipher had hacked the security feeds, Sarah had mapped the guards' rotations, and Jonah had held the fragile thread of their alliance together. They weren't a team, not really just three jagged pieces forced into alignment by a shared enemy. And now, with Kane's brains painting his throne, that thread was fraying.

The SUV slowed, weaving into a warren of backstreets, the city's underbelly swallowing them whole. Cipher drove with the same cold precision they'd shown in the penthouse, their hands steady on the wheel, their silence a wall Jonah couldn't breach. Who were they, really? A mercenary? A vigilante? Every answer Jonah grasped at slipped away, but one truth held: Cipher had pulled the trigger on Kane without hesitation, a choice Jonah hadn't been ready to make.

Sarah shifted, her shoulder brushing his, and he felt the tremor in her frame. "I didn't want to," she murmured, so quiet he almost missed it. "Hale he gave me no choice."

Jonah's throat tightened, words sticking like gravel. "I know."

But did he? Hale's betrayal had gutted him, a knife twisted by years of trust, but Sarah's shot had ended it saved him. He should've been grateful, should've felt something beyond this hollow ache, but all he could see was Hale's body hitting the floor, Sarah's hands shaking as she lowered the gun.

"He was going to kill you," she said, louder now, as if convincing herself. "I saw it in his eyes. He wasn't the Hale we knew anymore."

Jonah squeezed her hand, the gesture automatic, empty. "He wasn't," he agreed, though the words tasted like ash. Hale had been a shield, a guide until he wasn't. Until Kane's poison had turned him into a stranger with a gun aimed at Jonah's heart.

The SUV jolted over a pothole, jarring Jonah back to the present. Cipher glanced at them again, their voice cutting through the haze. "We're not clear yet. Kane's people will be hunting us. We need to disappear."

"Where?" Sarah asked, her tone brittle, exhaustion bleeding through.

"Somewhere they won't look," Cipher replied, eyes on the road.

"I've got a place. Off the grid."

Jonah nodded, too tired to argue, too raw to care. The city blurred outside warehouses and tenements, flickering streetlights casting long, skeletal shadows. He'd spent his life fighting its corruption, clawing for justice in a place that devoured it whole. Tonight, they'd struck a blow, but it felt like punching fog satisfying for a moment, then gone.

The ledger still burned in his mind, its pages a map of rot stretching beyond Kane, beyond Hale, into corners he couldn't yet see. Overlord's unconscious bulk on the penthouse floor was proof enough the network lived, thrived, even with its figurehead dead. And Jonah knew, with a certainty that chilled him, that this was only the beginning.

Sarah leaned against him, her head on his shoulder, her breathing uneven. "What now?" she whispered.

Jonah stared out at the city, its lights a constellation of lies. "We keep going," he said, his voice steady despite the storm inside. "Until it's done."

Cipher's hands tightened on the wheel, the SUV slipping deeper into the night. The reckoning had come, and they'd paid for it in blood and trust. But the city didn't sleep, didn't forgive and neither would they.

———————————————————

Hours later, the safehouse emerged from the darkness a squat, unmarked building on the edge of the industrial district, its windows boarded, its walls stained with rust and time. Cipher killed the engine, the silence sudden and oppressive. Jonah stepped out, the cold biting through his jacket, the air heavy with the stench of oil and decay.

Inside, the place was bare: concrete floors, a single bulb swaying from the ceiling, a table littered with maps and gear. Cipher moved with purpose, unpacking a duffel ammo, a laptop, a burner phone while Sarah sank into a chair, her face buried in her hands.

Jonah paced, his boots scuffing the floor, his mind a tangle of rage and grief. Hale's face flashed behind his eyes stern lectures in the precinct, quiet nods over whiskey after a bad case. Gone. All of it, gone. And Sarah she'd borne the weight of that loss, her loyalty to Jonah carved in the shape of a bullet.

Cipher powered up the laptop, their fingers flying over the keys. "Kane's death will ripple," they said, not looking up. "His lieutenants will scramble some to take his place, others to cut losses. We've got a window before they regroup."

"How long?" Jonah asked, his voice hoarse.

"Days, maybe. Depends how deep the ledger cuts." Cipher's eyes flicked to him, sharp and assessing. "You ready for what's next?"

Jonah met their gaze, the question hanging between them. Was he? He'd lost more tonight than he could name Hale, a piece of himself, the fragile hope that the city could be saved. But Kane's blood on that glass table was a start, a crack in the machine he'd sworn to dismantle.

"Yeah," he said, the word heavy, final. "I'm ready."

Sarah lifted her head, her eyes red but fierce. "Me too."

Cipher nodded, a ghost of approval in their stance, and turned back to the screen. The safehouse hummed with tension, a fragile sanctuary in a city that wanted them dead. Outside, the night pressed close, the beast stirring, its claws still sharp.

Jonah sat beside Sarah, their shoulders touching, the silence between them thick with unspoken promises. The reckoning had cost them everything trust, blood, the last threads of who they'd been. But it had also forged them anew, three blades tempered in fire, ready to cut deeper.

The war wasn't over. It was just beginning.

Chapter 5: Shadows of Trust

The safehouse was a crypt of neglect, a basement flat beneath a sagging tenement where the air hung heavy with mildew and the ghosts of forgotten lives. A single bulb dangled from a frayed cord, its light stuttering across walls stained with time, throwing jagged shadows over the scarred table where Jonah Raines sat. His broad frame slouched, his face a map of stubble and exhaustion, he stared at the laptop screen until the glow burned into his retinas. Across from him, Elena Morales paced, her boots scuffing the cracked linoleum, her sharp mind slicing through the silence with restless energy.

"Jonah, look at this," Elena said, her voice a blade cutting through the gloom. She tapped the screen, pulling up a file from the blood ledger a tangle of numbers and names they'd pried from Kane's empire. "It's a payment trail. Offshore accounts, laundered through dummy corporations. And it all points to one man."

Jonah leaned in, his bloodshot eyes narrowing. "Who?"

"Marcus Vale," she said, the name dropping like a stone into still water. "District Attorney Marcus Vale."

The words hit Jonah hard, a sucker punch to a gut already bruised by betrayal. Vale polished, poised, the city's golden boy in a tailored suit had been a fixture in Jonah's old life, a man he'd once nodded to in precinct halls, a man he'd thought stood for something. "Vale?" he rasped, disbelief threading his voice. "Kane's successor?"

Elena nodded, her fingers tracing the data. "He's been on the take for years burying cases, rigging juries, keeping Kane's machine oiled. And now, with Kane dead, he's moving to claim the throne. Look here transfers spiked after the confrontation. He's consolidating power, fast."

Jonah's hands curled into fists, nails digging into his palms. "A new power grab," he muttered, the pieces snapping into place. Kane's death hadn't ended the war it had just shifted the battlefield. "If Vale's running this, he's got the whole damn system in his pocket."

"We need more," Elena said, her tone urgent. "Plans, dates something concrete to nail him."

Jonah nodded, though his mind was a storm of rage and fatigue. "Keep digging. I'll get us coffee. We're not stopping till we've got him cold."

He stood, his joints creaking like old wood, and shuffled to the corner where a battered pot hissed on a hotplate. The bitter scent grounded him, a tether to the moment as he poured two mugs, the steam curling up like specters in the dimness. He handed one to Elena, their fingers brushing a fleeting warmth in a world gone cold.

Hours bled into the night, the safehouse a cocoon of tension. Jonah pored over the files beside Elena, decrypting messages, following money trails that snaked through the city's underbelly. Each revelation tightened the noose around Vale: a meeting with councilmen slated for next week, a payoff to silence a witness, a plan to strong-arm a rival faction into submission. The ledger was a confession in code, and they were its translators.

Dawn was a gray smear on the horizon when the burner phone buzzed, jolting Jonah from a haze of numbers. He snatched it up, reading the text: *Meet me. Pier 17. Now. -C*

"Cipher," he said, pocketing the phone. He grabbed his jacket, the leather creaking as he shrugged it on.

Elena looked up, worry etching her face. "You trust them?"

"Don't have a choice," Jonah replied, his voice gravel. "They've saved my ass twice. If they've got something on Vale, I need to hear it."

She didn't argue, just nodded, her eyes holding his for a beat longer than necessary. "Watch your back."

Jonah stepped into the morning, the city waking around him horns bleating, garbage trucks rumbling, the air thick with exhaust and salt from the nearby docks. Pier 17 was a rusted skeleton, its planks warped by years of neglect, the water below a sluggish black mirror. Cipher stood at the edge, their silver hair a beacon against the gloom, their coat whipping in the wind.

"You're late," Cipher said, their voice a low rasp, eyes hidden beneath the hood.

"Had to shake a shadow," Jonah lied, scanning the pier for threats. "What've you got?"

Cipher handed him a folded paper, the edges worn. "Read it."

Jonah unfolded it a photocopy of a handwritten note, the ink smudged but legible. *Vale's orders: Raines is a loose end. Use S to bait him. Eliminate both.* His stomach dropped, the initials searing into his brain. "S... Sarah?"

Cipher nodded, their gaze unyielding. "She's been feeding Vale intel since Hale turned. She's his mole."

The world tilted, Jonah's breath catching in his throat. Sarah his partner, his shield, the woman who'd put a bullet in Hale to save him a traitor? "No," he said, shaking his head. "She wouldn't. Not after everything."

"She did," Cipher said, stepping closer. "And she's coming for you now."

As if on cue, a shadow moved a figure slipping from behind a stack of crates, blonde hair glinting in the weak light. Sarah. Her service pistol gleamed in her hand, her face a mask of resolve and regret. "Jonah," she called, her voice steady despite the tremor in her stance. "I didn't want it to be like this."

He drew his own gun, instincts warring with memory. "Then why is it?"

"Vale had leverage," she said, her eyes glistening. "My sister Carla. He'd kill her if I didn't play along. I had no choice."

"There's always a choice," Jonah growled, his finger tightening on the trigger. "You sold us out."

Before she could respond, a shot cracked the air not from Sarah, but from Cipher. The bullet grazed her arm, sending her gun clattering to the pier. She stumbled, clutching the wound, and Cipher lunged, pinning her down with a knee to her chest.

"Move," Cipher barked at Jonah, dragging Sarah toward a rusted railing. "She's not alone."

Headlights flared in the distance, engines roaring closer Vale's men, closing the trap. Jonah hesitated, Sarah's pained gasp echoing in his ears, but Cipher hauled her up, shoving her toward him. "Take her. We're gone."

They ran, Sarah staggering between them, blood staining her sleeve. The pier blurred past, the pursuit gaining, until they reached a side street where Elena waited in a beat-up sedan. She flung the door open, eyes wide. "Get in!"

Jonah shoved Sarah into the back, piling in beside her as Cipher took the front. Elena gunned the engine, tires squealing as they tore into the city's maze, the headlights fading behind them.

The new safehouse was a squat garage on the edge of town, its walls lined with tools and oil stains, the air thick with gasoline fumes. Sarah sat on a crate, her arm bandaged with a rag, her face pale but defiant. Jonah loomed over her, fury simmering beneath his exhaustion.

"Talk," he said, his voice a low growl. "Everything."

Sarah met his gaze, her jaw tight. "Vale took over after Kane. He's been planning this for months new alliances, bigger payoffs. I was his eyes on you, feeding him your moves. But I swear, Jonah, I didn't want you dead."

"You expect me to believe that?" he snapped, pacing. "After Hale, after all we've been through?"

"She's telling the truth," Cipher cut in, leaning against the wall, arms crossed. "I've been tracking Vale's comms. She was a pawn coerced, not loyal."

Elena emerged from the shadows, her laptop balanced on a workbench. "Doesn't matter why. We've got bigger problems. Vale's office it's where he keeps the real dirt. Plans, names, evidence. If we hit it, we can end him."

Jonah stopped, his mind racing. "A raid. Risky as hell."

"No choice," Elena said, her tone steel. "He's tightening the net. We don't act, we're dead anyway."

Sarah's voice was quiet, strained. "I can get you in. Backdoor access maintenance codes. It's the least I can do."

Jonah studied her, the trust he'd once had fractured beyond repair. But necessity outweighed doubt. "Fine. You're with us. One wrong move, Sarah, and I won't hesitate."

She nodded, a flicker of shame crossing her face. "Understood."

The plan came together in hours, a desperate gamble forged in the garage's dim light. Sarah provided the codes, Elena mapped the office layout, and Cipher scouted the perimeter via a stolen drone feed. By midnight, they were ready three shadows in a city that never slept.

Vale's office sat atop a glass tower downtown, a monument to power and deceit. They slipped in through a service entrance, Sarah's codes disarming the locks, their footsteps muffled on the tiled floor. The elevator hummed as it carried them up, the tension thick enough to choke on.

The office was a fortress of luxury polished wood, leather chairs, a panoramic view of the skyline twinkling below. Vale stood at his desk, a silhouette against the city lights, his silver hair gleaming as he turned. Two guards flanked him, guns drawn, their faces hard with purpose.

"Raines," Vale said, his voice smooth as venom. "You're persistent, I'll give you that."

Jonah leveled his pistol, his aim steady. "It's over, Vale. We've got the ledger. We know everything."

Vale laughed, a cold, hollow sound. "You think that matters? This city's mine. You're just a cockroach I haven't stomped yet."

The guards advanced, but Cipher moved faster a blur of motion, two shots dropping them in their tracks. Vale's smirk faltered, his hand darting for a drawer, but Jonah was on him, slamming him against the desk, the gun pressed to his temple.

"Endgame," Jonah said, his voice ice. "Where's the evidence?"

Vale sneered, blood trickling from a split lip. "You'll never "

Cipher fired, the bullet punching through Vale's chest. He slumped, eyes wide with shock, then crumpled to the floor, a puppet with cut strings. Jonah stared, the suddenness of it jarring, but there was no time for regret.

"Over here," Elena called, cracking the desk's hidden panel. She pulled out a hard drive, its surface glinting in the dimness. "This is it financials, recordings, the works."

Alarms shrieked, red lights pulsing as security systems kicked in. "Move!" Cipher shouted, kicking the door open. They ran, the hard drive clutched in Elena's hands, down stairwells and through corridors, boots pounding concrete as guards closed in.

A bullet whizzed past Jonah's head, splintering plaster. He returned fire, dropping a pursuer, while Cipher cleared the path ahead. Sarah lagged, her wound slowing her, but she kept pace, her face set with determination.

They burst into the night, piling into the sedan as sirens wailed in the distance. Elena floored it, weaving through traffic, the tower receding behind them like a bad dream. The safehouse welcomed them back, its shadows a refuge as they collapsed, breathless and alive.

Elena plugged the hard drive in, her screen filling with files ledgers within ledgers, audio of Vale's deals, a blueprint of corruption so vast it staggered the mind. "This'll bury them," she said, her voice trembling with triumph. "All of them."

Jonah stood by the window, the city's lights a distant pulse. Sarah's betrayal gnawed at him, a wound deeper than any bullet. "You knew," he said, turning to her. "You could've warned us."

"I tried," she whispered, her eyes downcast. "But Vale had Carla. I was trapped."

Cipher watched from the corner, their silence a judgment Jonah couldn't read. "She's out now," they said finally. "Vale's dead. Her leash is cut."

Jonah nodded, the weight of it settling in. They'd won a battle, secured the evidence to shake the city's foundations, but the cost was etched in every line of his face trust shattered, a partner lost to the shadows.

Elena closed the laptop, her gaze meeting his. "We're not done. This is just the start."

"Yeah," Jonah said, his voice low, resolute. "It's a war. And we're still in it."

The night stretched on, the hard drive's secrets poised to ignite a reckoning. Jonah lit a cigarette, the smoke curling upward, a fleeting ghost in a room thick with purpose. Vale was gone, but the machine he'd served still churned, and Jonah knew the fight was far from over. With Elena and Cipher beside him, he'd see it through no matter how deep the shadows grew.

The hours blurred, the safehouse a bunker against the chaos outside. Jonah replayed the raid in his mind the gunfire, Vale's last gasp, the weight of the hard drive in Elena's hands. It was a victory, but it felt like a pyrrhic one, the taste of ash lingering beneath the adrenaline.

Sarah sat apart, her bandaged arm a stark reminder of her divided loyalties. "What happens to me now?" she asked, her voice small.

Jonah didn't answer right away, the silence heavy. "You're out," he said finally. "You've got blood on your hands, same as us. But you don't get a say anymore."

She nodded, accepting it, her eyes hollow. "Carla's safe?"

"Ramirez has her," Elena said, glancing up from her notes. "Protective custody. She'll testify if it comes to it."

Relief flickered across Sarah's face, a brief light in the dark. "Thank you."

"Don't," Jonah said, his tone flat. "This isn't forgiveness."

Cipher broke the tension, stepping forward. "We need to move soon. Vale's death'll stir the hornets. They'll hunt us harder now."

Jonah exhaled, the cigarette's ember flaring. "Let them come. We've got the ammo to hit back."

Elena began encrypting the files, her fingers a steady rhythm against the keys. "By morning, this goes live. Every outlet, every contact I've got. The city won't sleep through this."

The plan was set, the die cast. Jonah watched the skyline, its towers glinting like knives in the night, a city teetering on the edge of collapse or redemption. He'd lost too much to turn back Hale, Sarah, pieces of himself but the fight burned in him still, a fire fed by rage and a stubborn flicker of hope.

Cipher joined him at the window, their presence a quiet anchor. "You're still standing," they said, a rare softness in their rasp.

"Barely," Jonah replied, the ghost of a smile tugging at his lips. "But yeah."

The dawn would bring chaos, a reckoning long overdue. With Elena's truth and Cipher's steel, Jonah faced it head-on, a rogue in a war without end, chasing justice through the shadows of trust.

The cigarette burned down to the filter, and Jonah crushed it under his boot, the act a small rebellion against the weight pressing on his chest. Elena's laptop hummed, the files uploading to a dozen secure servers, a digital wildfire ready to spread. Sarah curled into herself, a shadow of the partner he'd known, while Cipher cleaned their rifle with methodical precision, each click a promise of battles to come.

Jonah's mind drifted to the ledger, its secrets now a weapon in their hands. Vale's death was a blow, but the system he'd served was a hydra cut one head, and another would rise. The evidence would spark arrests, protests, maybe even change, but Jonah wasn't naive enough to think it'd be clean or quick.

"You think this'll stick?" he asked Elena, his voice rough.

She didn't look up, her focus absolute. "It'll stick if we make it. People want a fight they just need a reason. This is it."

He nodded, her certainty a lifeline. The city was a beast, wounded but not dead, and they were its hunters now, stalking its dark veins for the next strike. Sarah's betrayal had carved a hollow in him, but it also sharpened his edge, a reminder that trust was a luxury he'd traded for survival.

Cipher slung the rifle over their shoulder, meeting his gaze. "Next move's yours, Raines."

Jonah turned back to the window, the first rays of dawn painting the sky in streaks of fire. "We keep going," he said, the words a vow. "Till it's done."

The safehouse fell silent, the weight of their purpose settling over them like a shroud. The evidence was secure, Vale was dead, and the war stretched out before them, a gauntlet of shadows and blood. Jonah embraced it, his resolve a blade forged in loss, ready to cut deeper into the heart of a city that had betrayed them all.

Chapter 6: The Fallout

The safehouse was a relic of better days, a forgotten apartment tucked away in a crumbling building on the city's edge. Jonah pushed the door open, its hinges groaning in protest, and stepped into the stale air. The place smelled of dust and old wood, with a faint undertone of something sour maybe a long-abandoned meal or a leak in the plumbing. He flicked the light switch, and a single bulb buzzed to life, casting a weak glow over the room. The walls were peeling, the wallpaper curling back like dead skin, and the floorboards creaked under his boots as he moved inside.

Elena followed him in, her laptop clutched to her chest like a shield. Cipher slipped in last, their movements silent, their eyes scanning the space with practiced efficiency. The door clicked shut behind them, sealing them into this temporary sanctuary. Jonah dropped his duffel bag onto a sagging couch, the springs groaning under the weight. He ran a hand through his hair, the grit of the night's chaos still clinging to him, and exhaled slowly, trying to shake off the tension coiled in his muscles.

Elena set her laptop on a rickety table, its surface scarred with cigarette burns and water rings. She plugged it in, the screen flickering to life, casting a blue glow over her determined face. "I need to get these files out," she said, her voice steady despite the exhaustion etched into her features. "The ledger, Vale's recordings everything. If I can upload them to my contacts, we can blow this wide open."

Jonah nodded, his jaw tight. "Do it. But be careful. They'll be watching for any trace."

Cipher moved to the window, peering through the grimy blinds at the street below. "We're clear for now," they said, their voice a low rasp. "But we can't stay long. Vale's people will be hunting us."

Jonah sank into a chair, its wooden frame creaking ominously. He rubbed his temples, the weight of the past days pressing down on him like a physical force. Sarah's face flashed in his mind her tear-streaked cheeks, the tremor in her voice as she confessed her betrayal. He'd sent her away, told her to disappear, but the ache of her absence was a raw wound, festering with every breath. And Carla God, Carla. Last he'd heard, she was in protective custody, but with Vale's network still active, who knew how safe she really was?

He pulled out his burner phone, checking for messages. Nothing. Ramirez had promised to keep him updated, but the silence was deafening. Jonah's fingers itched to call, to demand answers, but he knew better. Every contact was a risk, every connection a potential thread for their enemies to pull.

Elena's fingers flew over the keyboard, her brow furrowed in concentration. "I'm routing through a VPN, bouncing the signal. It'll take time, but it should keep us hidden."

Jonah watched her work, marveling at her focus. She was a force of nature, a journalist who'd traded safety for truth, and he admired her for it. But admiration didn't dull the edge of his worry. "How long?" he asked.

"An hour, maybe two," she replied, not looking up. "Depends on the file sizes and the connection."

He nodded, though impatience gnawed at him. Two hours felt like an eternity when every second could bring danger to their door. Cipher remained by the window, a sentinel in the gloom, their presence both reassuring and unsettling. Jonah still didn't know what to make of them ally or enigma, their motives shrouded in shadow.

He stood, pacing the small room, his boots scuffing the worn floor. The safehouse was a cage, its walls closing in with every lap. He needed air, needed to think, but stepping outside was suicide. Instead, he retreated to a corner, leaning against the wall, his mind churning.

Sarah. The name was a splinter under his skin. He'd trusted her, fought beside her, shared pieces of himself he'd kept locked away. And she'd sold him out, fed Vale his every move. Part of him understood Vale had leverage, had threatened Carla, and Sarah had been trapped. But understanding didn't erase the betrayal, didn't mend the fracture in his chest. She'd chosen her sister over him, over their partnership, and that choice had nearly gotten them all killed.

A memory surfaced, unbidden: Sarah laughing over coffee in the precinct break room, her eyes bright with a joke he'd forgotten. They'd been friends once, before the ledger, before Kane's shadow swallowed their lives. Now, that friendship was ash, scattered by the winds of deceit.

And Carla young, scared, caught in a web not of her making. Jonah had pressured her for information, used her as a pawn in his crusade, and now she was paying the price. If Vale's people got to her, if they silenced her before she could testify... He clenched his fists, the guilt a lead weight in his gut.

"Jonah," Elena's voice cut through his thoughts. "You okay?"

He blinked, realizing he'd been staring at the wall. "Yeah," he lied, forcing a nod. "Just thinking."

She studied him, her gaze piercing. "About Sarah?"

He flinched, the name a lash. "And Carla. I dragged them into this mess."

Elena's expression softened, a rare crack in her armor. "You didn't drag them. They made choices, same as us. Sarah chose to protect her sister, even if it meant betraying you. Carla chose to help, knowing the risks. We're all in this together, for better or worse."

Jonah wanted to believe her, but the doubt lingered, a poison seeping through his veins. "Doesn't make it easier," he muttered.

"No," she agreed, turning back to her laptop. "But it's the hand we're dealt."

Time crawled, each minute a slow drip of tension. Jonah busied himself checking their gear, cleaning his pistol with mechanical precision, the familiar routine a balm for his frayed nerves. Cipher remained vigilant, their eyes never leaving the street below. The safehouse was a bubble of uneasy calm, the world outside poised on the brink of explosion.

Finally, Elena leaned back, a sigh escaping her lips. "It's done," she said, her voice tinged with relief. "The files are uploaded. My contacts are disseminating them as we speak."

Jonah's heart quickened, a mix of anticipation and dread. "How long before it hits?"

"Minutes," she replied, closing the laptop. "The news cycle moves fast. By morning, it'll be everywhere."

He nodded, the reality of it sinking in. They'd fired the first shot in a war that would shake the city to its core. Protests, arrests, chaos it was all coming, a storm they'd unleashed. But with it came exposure, a spotlight that could burn them as easily as their enemies.

Cipher turned from the window, their face half-lit by the bulb's weak glow. "We should move soon. Once the news breaks, this place won't be safe."

Jonah agreed, but the thought of uprooting again, of running when his body screamed for rest, was a weight he could barely shoulder. "Where to?" he asked.

"I've got a spot," Cipher said, their tone clipped. "An old warehouse, off the grid. We can lay low there until the heat dies down."

Elena began packing her gear, her movements efficient despite the fatigue etched into her face. Jonah helped, stowing the laptop and their scant supplies into duffel bags. The safehouse had served its purpose, but it was time to vanish once more.

As they prepared to leave, the small TV in the corner flickered to life, its screen crackling with static before resolving into a news broadcast. A stern-faced anchor sat behind a desk, the headline scrolling beneath her: "Breaking: Massive Corruption Scandal Rocks City Hall."

Jonah froze, his breath catching. It was happening.

"Sources have leaked a trove of documents implicating high-ranking officials in a web of bribery, extortion, and murder," the anchor intoned, her voice grave. "Among those named are Deputy Chief Alvarez, Councilman Greer, and the late District Attorney Marcus Vale. Arrests are underway, and protests are erupting across the city as citizens demand accountability."

The screen cut to footage of angry crowds outside city hall, their signs waving like flags of war. Police in riot gear stood tense, batons at the ready, as chants of "Justice now!" echoed through the streets. Another clip showed officers leading a handcuffed man Jonah recognized him as a precinct captain into a squad car, his face a mask of disbelief.

Elena's hand found Jonah's arm, her grip tight. "We did it," she whispered, a tremor of awe in her voice.

But Jonah's eyes were glued to the screen, his mind racing. This was just the beginning. The ledger's revelations would topple careers, shatter lives, but Kane's network was a hydra cut one head, and two more would grow. The real power players, the ones who'd stayed in the shadows, would be scrambling to cover their tracks, to eliminate threats. And Jonah and his allies were at the top of that list.

His burner phone buzzed in his pocket, startling him. He pulled it out, the screen displaying a single message from Ramirez: *Meet me. Old diner on 5th. Urgent.*

Jonah's gut tightened. Ramirez was their lifeline in the bureau, a rare honest agent in a sea of corruption. If she was reaching out now, it was serious.

"I've got to go," he said, slipping the phone back into his pocket. "Ramirez needs to see me."

Elena's brow furrowed. "Now? It's dangerous out there."

"More dangerous not to know what she's got," Jonah replied, grabbing his jacket. "I'll be quick. You two head to the warehouse. I'll meet you there."

Cipher nodded, their expression unreadable. "Watch your six. The streets are a powder keg."

Jonah gave a curt nod and slipped out the door, the night air hitting him like a slap. The city was alive with unrest, distant sirens wailing, the glow of fires painting the horizon in angry reds and oranges. He kept to the shadows, his hood pulled low, every sense on high alert.

The diner on 5th was a relic, its neon sign flickering sporadically, the windows steamed from the heat inside. Jonah pushed through the door, the bell jingling faintly. The place was nearly empty, save for a lone waitress wiping down counters and Ramirez sitting in a corner booth, her dark suit rumpled, her eyes shadowed with fatigue.

He slid into the seat across from her, the vinyl creaking under his weight. "You look like hell," he said by way of greeting.

Ramirez managed a weak smile, her lips thin. "Feel like it too. The bureau's in chaos. Half the agents are celebrating, popping champagne like we've won the war. The other half are scrambling to cover their asses, praying their names don't show up in that damn ledger."

Jonah signaled for coffee, the waitress shuffling over with a pot that looked older than the diner. "What's the fallout?" he asked, keeping his voice low.

"Arrests are happening," Ramirez said, leaning back, her fingers drumming a restless rhythm on the table. "Politicians, cops, even some feds who got too cozy with Kane's payroll. But it's messy. His network's fighting back lawyering up, making threats, calling in favors. It's going to be a long fight, Raines."

Jonah's stomach tightened, a knot of tension he couldn't shake. "And Carla?" he asked, his voice tightening at the mention of her name.

Ramirez's expression softened with regret, her eyes dropping to the table. "She's in protective custody, but it's precarious. Vale's people are still out there, and they're not above hitting witnesses. We're doing our best, but..." She trailed off, the unspoken danger hanging heavy between them.

Jonah's fists clenched under the table, his knuckles white. "She's just a kid. She didn't ask for any of this."

"I know," Ramirez said quietly. "We'll keep her safe. But you need to watch your back too. Kane's lieutenants are regrouping, and they'll be looking for payback. You're at the top of their list."

Jonah nodded, the warning settling like ice in his veins. "I'm used to it," he said, though the truth was, he was bone-tired, the fight wearing him down to raw edges.

Ramirez studied him, her gaze piercing. "Don't get cocky, Jonah. This isn't over. Not by a long shot."

He met her eyes, a flicker of defiance sparking through his exhaustion. "I know. But we've got momentum. The city's waking up. We can't stop now."

She sighed, a weary sound. "Just be careful. You're playing a dangerous game, and the stakes are life and death."

The waitress returned with his coffee, the mug chipped and stained. Jonah took a sip, the bitter liquid scalding his throat. "I'll manage," he said, setting the cup down. "Thanks for the heads-up."

Ramirez nodded, standing to leave. "Stay in touch. And Jonah don't trust anyone. Not even me."

He watched her go, her words echoing in his mind. Trust was a currency he couldn't afford, not anymore. With Sarah's betrayal still fresh, every alliance felt like a potential knife in the back.

Back at the warehouse, the air was thick with the scent of oil and rust, the cavernous space echoing with their footsteps. Elena had set up her laptop on a workbench, monitoring the news feeds, while Cipher prowled the perimeter, their rifle slung over their shoulder.

Jonah dropped into a chair, his body protesting the movement. "Ramirez says Kane's people are still active. We're not out of the woods yet."

Elena looked up, her face grim. "The protests are growing. They've shut down half the city. But the pushback is fierce. Some of the arrested officials are already out on bail, lawyering up."

Jonah rubbed his eyes, the weight of it all pressing down. "We knew it wouldn't be easy. But we've got the truth on our side. That's something."

Cipher's voice cut through the gloom, sharp and pragmatic. "Truth's a weapon, but it's not armor. We need to stay sharp, stay hidden."

Jonah nodded, his resolve hardening. "We will. We've come too far to back down now."

Elena's laptop pinged, a new alert flashing on the screen. "Another arrest," she said, scanning the update. "Chief Hargrove. They're taking him in now."

Jonah leaned forward, a grim satisfaction settling in his chest. Hargrove had been a thorn in his side for years, a bureaucrat more interested in politics than justice. Seeing him fall was a small victory, but a victory nonetheless.

The hours stretched, the warehouse a cocoon of tension and fatigue. Jonah's thoughts drifted back to Sarah, to the last words they'd exchanged her tearful apology, his cold dismissal. He'd sent her away to protect her, to protect himself, but the void she'd left was a constant ache.

And Carla trapped in a system that had failed her, her future hanging by a thread. Jonah had promised to keep her safe, but promises were fragile things in a city like this.

As night fell, the warehouse's shadows deepened, the city's unrest a distant roar. Jonah stood by a cracked window, staring out at the skyline, its towers aglow with a false promise of order. The fight was far from over, the cost already steep, but he couldn't turn back. Not now. Not ever.

Elena joined him, her presence a quiet comfort. "We're making a difference," she said softly. "It's messy, but it's real."

Jonah glanced at her, the fire in her eyes a mirror of his own. "Yeah," he said, his voice rough with emotion. "And we'll keep going. No matter what."

Cipher's silhouette loomed in the background, a guardian in the dark. Together, they were a fractured alliance, bound by purpose and peril. The fallout was just beginning, and Jonah knew the road ahead would be brutal. But he was ready. For Sarah, for Carla, for the city he'd sworn to protect he'd see this through to the end.

The warehouse creaked around them, a symphony of old metal and whispered drafts. Jonah lit a cigarette, the flare of the match briefly illuminating his haggard face. He inhaled deeply, the smoke curling upward, a fleeting ghost in the stillness. Elena returned to her laptop, her fingers tapping out messages to her network, ensuring the ledger's revelations spread like wildfire.

Cipher approached, their steps silent, their eyes glinting in the dim light. "You should rest," they said, their tone almost gentle. "Tomorrow brings new battles."

Jonah exhaled a plume of smoke, his gaze distant. "Can't sleep. Too much noise in my head."

Cipher nodded, understanding without words. "The fight takes its toll. But you're still standing. That's something."

Jonah managed a faint smile, the gesture foreign on his lips. "Barely. But yeah."

They stood together in silence, two warriors in a war without end, the city's heartbeat thrumming through the walls. The fallout was a storm, raging beyond their sanctuary, but within these walls, they found a moment of respite, a breath before the plunge.

Jonah crushed the cigarette under his boot, the ember dying with a hiss. "Let's get some shut-eye," he said, turning to Elena. "We'll need it."

She nodded, closing her laptop with a decisive click. "Tomorrow, we keep pushing."

As they settled onto makeshift beds blankets on the concrete floor the warehouse enveloped them in its embrace, a fragile haven in a world gone mad. Jonah lay awake, staring at the ceiling, the echoes of the day replaying in his mind. Sarah's face, Carla's fear, Ramirez's warning it all swirled together, a tempest of doubt and determination.

But beneath it all, a spark remained a stubborn flicker of hope that refused to die. They'd struck a blow, and the city was reeling. It wasn't victory, not yet, but it was a start. And for Jonah Raines, that was enough to keep fighting.

He closed his eyes, the darkness a welcome shroud, and let sleep claim him, if only for a while. The war would wait, but not for long.

The next morning dawned gray and heavy, the sky a slab of concrete pressing down on the city. Jonah woke to the sound of rain tapping against the warehouse roof, a steady rhythm that matched the ache in his bones. He sat up, his muscles protesting, and rubbed the sleep from his eyes.

Elena was already awake, hunched over her laptop, a mug of instant coffee steaming beside her. Cipher stood by the door, their rifle cradled in their arms, ever vigilant.

"Morning," Jonah grunted, his voice rough with disuse.

Elena glanced up, offering a tired smile. "Morning. The news is exploding. More arrests, more protests. They're calling it the purge of the century."

Jonah nodded, a grim satisfaction settling in his chest. "Good. Let it burn."

But even as he spoke, Ramirez's warning echoed in his mind. The fight wasn't over; it was evolving, the shadows regrouping for the next strike. He knew they couldn't rest on their laurels complacency was death in this game.

He stood, stretching his stiff limbs, and joined Elena at the workbench. "What's next?" he asked.

She tapped the screen, pulling up a map dotted with red pins. "These are known Kane safehouses and stash points. If we can hit them, disrupt their operations, we can keep them on the back foot."

Jonah studied the map, his mind already plotting routes and risks. "It's a start. But we need intel something to give us an edge."

Cipher's voice cut through the air, sharp and clear. "I've got contacts. Whispers from the underworld. There's a meeting tonight Kane's lieutenants, scrambling to fill the void. If we can intercept, we might learn their next move."

Jonah turned, his interest piqued. "Where?"

"An old factory on the docks," Cipher replied. "Heavily guarded, but I can get us in."

Elena's eyes lit up, the thrill of the hunt sparking within her. "We could plant bugs, record their plans. Turn their own words against them."

Jonah nodded, the plan taking shape. "It's risky, but it's a chance we can't pass up."

They spent the day preparing gathering gear, studying blueprints, honing their strategy. The warehouse buzzed with a renewed sense of purpose, the air thick with anticipation. Jonah felt the familiar surge of adrenaline, the call to action that had driven him through countless battles.

As night fell, they donned their gear black clothes, concealed weapons, faces set with determination. The city awaited, a labyrinth of danger and opportunity, and they were ready to plunge into its depths once more.

Jonah checked his pistol, the weight reassuring in his hand. He glanced at Elena and Cipher, their resolve mirroring his own. "Let's do this," he said, his voice steady.

Together, they stepped out into the rain-slicked streets, shadows among shadows, hunters in a city that never slept. The fallout had begun, but their fight was far from over. With every step, Jonah felt the weight of his choices, the cost of his crusade, but he pressed on, driven by a fire that refused to be quenched.

For Sarah, for Carla, for the city he loved and hated in equal measure he would see this through to the end. No matter the cost.

The factory loomed ahead, a hulking silhouette against the

night sky, its windows dark and foreboding. Jonah led the way, his senses on high alert, every nerve attuned to the dangers that lurked within. Elena and Cipher flanked him, their movements synchronized, a well-oiled machine forged in the crucible of conflict.

They slipped through a side entrance, the door hanging crooked on its hinges, and into the cavernous interior. The air was thick with the scent of rust and decay, the floor littered with debris. Jonah's flashlight cut through the darkness, illuminating their path as they navigated the maze of abandoned machinery.

According to Cipher's intel, the meeting was set for the foreman's office on the second floor. They climbed a rickety staircase, each step creaking ominously, and positioned themselves in the shadows outside the office door.

Voices drifted from within, low and tense. Jonah strained to listen, catching fragments of conversation names, plans, the scramble for power in the wake of Vale's demise. Elena set up her recording equipment, her hands steady despite the adrenaline coursing through her.

As the meeting progressed, the lieutenants' voices grew heated, arguments flaring over territory and resources. Jonah's mind raced, cataloging every word, every nuance. This was gold evidence that could cripple Kane's network, expose their fractures.

But then, a new voice cut through the din a familiar one that sent ice down Jonah's spine. "Enough bickering," the voice said, commanding and cold. "We have a common enemy. Raines and his allies are still out there, and they won't stop until we're all in chains."

Jonah's blood ran cold. It was Overlord, Kane's right hand, the man who'd nearly killed him in the penthouse raid. He was alive, and he was rallying the troops.

Elena's eyes met Jonah's, wide with alarm. Cipher tensed, their hand drifting to their weapon. The stakes had just skyrocketed.

"We need to take him out," Jonah whispered, his voice barely audible.

Cipher shook their head. "Too many guards. We'd be slaughtered."

Elena's recorder whirred softly, capturing every damning word. "We've got what we need," she murmured. "Let's get out while we can."

But before they could move, the office door swung open, and Overlord stepped out, his massive frame filling the doorway. His eyes locked onto Jonah's, recognition sparking in their depths.

"Raines," he growled, a cruel smile twisting his lips. "You just can't stay dead, can you?"

Jonah's pistol snapped up, but Overlord was faster, lunging forward with startling speed. The two men collided, grappling in the narrow corridor, their struggle a brutal dance of fists and fury. Elena and Cipher sprang into action, engaging the guards who poured from the office, gunfire erupting in the confined space.

Jonah slammed Overlord against the wall, the impact jarring his bones, but the big man barely flinched. He drove his knee into Jonah's gut, doubling him over, then wrapped his hands around Jonah's throat, squeezing with merciless strength.

Stars exploded in Jonah's vision, his lungs screaming for air. He clawed at Overlord's grip, his fingers digging into flesh, but the man's hold was iron. Desperation clawed at him, and he fumbled for his backup knife, strapped to his ankle.

With a final surge of strength, he drew the blade and plunged it into Overlord's side, twisting viciously. The man roared, his grip loosening, and Jonah gasped for breath, shoving him back.

Overlord staggered, blood seeping through his shirt, his eyes blazing with rage. "You'll pay for that," he snarled, reaching for his gun.

But Cipher was there, their rifle barking once, the shot clean and final. Overlord's head snapped back, and he crumpled to the floor, a lifeless heap.

The remaining guards faltered, their leader fallen, and Elena took advantage of the chaos, dropping one with a well-placed shot. Jonah scrambled to his feet, his throat raw, his vision swimming, but he raised his pistol, covering their retreat.

"Go!" Cipher shouted, laying down suppressive fire as they backed toward the stairs.

They fled, the factory a blur of shadows and echoes, the night swallowing them whole. Behind them, the meeting lay in ruins, Kane's lieutenants scattered or dead, their plans in disarray.

***

Back at the warehouse, Jonah collapsed onto a crate, his body a tapestry of bruises and cuts. Elena tended to his wounds, her hands gentle but efficient, while Cipher stood watch, ever vigilant.

"We got lucky," Elena said, wrapping a bandage around Jonah's arm. "But we've got the recording. It's enough to keep the pressure on."

Jonah nodded, though his mind was elsewhere. Overlord's words haunted him *a common enemy*. Kane's network was uniting against them, a formidable force even in disarray. The fight was escalating, the dangers multiplying.

But they'd survived, struck another blow, and the city was stirring, its people awakening to the rot within. Jonah clung to that, a lifeline in the storm.

"We keep going," he said, his voice hoarse but resolute. "One step at a time."

Elena smiled, a flicker of warmth in the cold. "Together."

Cipher's silhouette loomed in the doorway, a guardian in the night. "Always."

The warehouse settled into silence, the city's pulse a distant thrum. Jonah closed his eyes, the weight of the day settling over him like a shroud. The fallout was a tempest, but they were the eye, calm and unyielding. And as long as they stood, the fight would continue.

For now, that was enough.

Chapter 7: The Ally

The parking garage loomed ahead, a squat fortress of concrete and shadow hunched against the city's skyline. Jonah Raines eased his battered sedan into a space on the third level, the engine's low growl fading into silence as he killed the ignition. The air hung heavy with the tang of exhaust and damp stone, the flickering fluorescents overhead casting a jaundiced glow that barely pierced the darkness. He sat still for a moment, hands tight on the wheel, his pulse a steady thud in his ears. Mike Daniels. The name churned in his gut, sharp and bitter, a splinter of betrayal lodged deep from the ledger's black-and-white truth.

He stepped out, the car door's slam ricocheting through the empty expanse like a gunshot. Old instincts flared his eyes swept the level, marking the exits, the pillars thick enough to shield a man if it came to that. The weight of the pistol at his hip was a cold comfort, a reminder of how far he'd fallen from the badge he'd once worn. He adjusted his jacket and moved toward the stairwell, boots scuffing softly against the grit-strewn floor. Each sound amplified in the stillness the drip of a unseen leak, the faint rumble of traffic beyond the walls, the creak of the building settling into its bones.

The fourth floor greeted him with deeper shadows, the lights here more sporadic, buzzing like trapped flies. A figure stood near a pillar, half-swallowed by the gloom. Mike. Even from twenty paces, Jonah could see the wear in him the slump of his shoulders, the nervous twitch of his hands as he fumbled with an unlit cigarette. He wasn't the man Jonah remembered, the one who'd shared coffee on graveyard shifts, who'd had his back when the streets turned ugly. This Mike looked hollowed out, a shell of guilt and exhaustion.

Jonah approached, deliberate, letting his footsteps announce him. Mike turned, his face catching the light pale, lined, eyes sunken with a weariness that went beyond sleepless nights. Fear flickered there too, a hunted look Jonah knew too well.

"Jonah," Mike rasped, voice rough as gravel. "You came."

"Had to," Jonah said, stopping short, his stance loose but ready. "Your name's all over the ledger, Mike. Bribes, drop-offs, Kane's dirty laundry. You're in it up to your neck."

Mike flinched, his gaze dropping to the stained concrete. "I know how it looks. What you must think."

"Don't care what I think." Jonah's voice cut sharp, edged with the anger he'd nursed since Elena cracked the ledger open. "I want why. You owed me that much."

Mike's hands shook as he sparked the cigarette, the flame trembling in the dimness. He took a drag, smoke curling upward, thin and gray as his excuses. "It wasn't supposed to go this far. Started small looking the other way, passing a message. They said it kept the balance, kept the city from eating itself alive."

Jonah's jaw tightened. "That's a piss-poor lie, even for you. People died, Mike. Cops, informants, civilians blood's on that ledger, and you signed it."

"I know!" Mike's voice broke, raw and ragged. He pressed a hand to his forehead, the cigarette smoldering between his fingers. "But they had me, Jonah. They had Emily."

Jonah froze, the name a punch to the chest. "Your girl?"

Mike nodded, eyes glistening, wet with shame and desperation. "Leukemia. Diagnosed two years back. Treatments cost more than I'll ever see, and the insurance laughed in my face. Kane's people they came to me, said they'd pay it all. Keep her alive. But I had to play their game."

The anger in Jonah faltered, cracking under a flood of something softer, something he didn't want to feel. Sympathy. He saw Emily in his mind's eye six years old, all pigtails and gap-toothed grins, the kid Mike used to bring to precinct picnics. "Christ, Mike. Why didn't you tell me? We could've "

"What?" Mike cut in, bitter. "Found a miracle? You were out there chasing ghosts, Jonah, and I was drowning. They didn't give me options they gave me orders. Cross them, and Emily's gone. Or worse."

Jonah scrubbed a hand over his face, the stubble rough against his palm. He wanted to hate Mike, to let the betrayal burn clean and bright, but the man in front of him was a wreck cornered, broken, a father who'd sold his soul for a hospital bill. "So you rolled over. Let them own you."

Mike's laugh was a choke, a sound of self-loathing. "Yeah. And now I'm a dead man walking either way."

Silence fell, heavy as the concrete around them. Jonah's mind churned, torn between the ledger's cold facts and the human cost staring him down. He'd seen coercion before Kane's machine thrived on it but this hit different. Personal. "I get it," he said finally, voice low. "Doesn't erase what you did. Or what I've got to do."

Mike straightened slightly, resignation settling over him like dust. "I figured. But maybe I can give you something. A stash house east side, near the docks. Kane kept his real dirt there, off the books. Ledgers, tapes, leverage. You get that, you might crack his whole damn empire."

Jonah's pulse quickened, the lead sparking a flicker of purpose. "Where?"

Mike opened his mouth, but a sharp *crack* split the air a sniper's shot. Blood sprayed from Mike's side, a dark bloom against his shirt as he staggered, clutching the pillar. "Down!" Jonah barked, diving behind a rusted pickup as more shots erupted, ricocheting off the concrete in a deadly hail.

He risked a glance, spotting two figures emerging from the stairwell black-clad, armed, moving with the precision of hired muscle. Kane's enforcers, no doubt, here to tie up loose ends. Jonah drew his pistol, the grip slick with sweat, and fired twice. One attacker grunted, dropping, but the other ducked behind a sedan, returning fire.

"Mike!" Jonah scrambled toward him, staying low. Mike was slumped now, breath coming in shallow gasps, his shirt soaked crimson. "Hang on "

"Too late," Mike wheezed, fumbling a small key from his pocket and pressing it into Jonah's hand. "Stash house... east side..." He shoved a crumpled note after it, fingers trembling. "Partial... find it..."

Bullets chewed the pillar above them, showering dust. Jonah fired back, buying seconds, but the second attacker was closing, and a third shadow loomed at the stairwell. "Come on, we're getting out "

"No," Mike rasped, shoving him weakly. "Go. Make it mean something." He raised his own gun with a shaking hand, firing at the advancing figure a distraction, a last stand.

Jonah's throat tightened, but he nodded, a silent promise. He squeezed Mike's shoulder, then bolted, weaving through the maze of cars as shots chased him, pinging off metal and glass. His boots pounded the concrete, lungs burning, the key and note clutched tight in his fist.

He hit the stairwell, taking the steps three at a time, the echoes of gunfire fading behind him. Mike's shots stopped silence, then a single, final crack. Jonah didn't look back. He burst onto the street, the night air cold and sharp, and melted into an alley, losing himself in the city's tangle.

Hours later, he sat in a motel room that stank of mildew and stale smoke, the neon sign outside buzzing through a cracked window. The key lay on the chipped table, small and brass, maybe for a lockbox or a safe. Beside it, the note creased, blood-smeared, the ink smudged from Mike's dying grip. *East side, docks, 47* The rest was illegible, a blur of numbers and letters that taunted him.

Jonah lit a cigarette, the flame steady despite the tremor in his chest. He exhaled, watching the smoke twist upward, gray and fleeting. Mike was gone. Another name scratched off the board, another friend lost to the rot eating this city alive. But he'd given Jonah something a thread, thin and frayed, but real.

He remembered Mike from the old days laughing over bad coffee, trading stories about busts gone sideways. A good cop, once. A father, always. The ledger hadn't shown that part, the human part, and now it never would. "You did what you could," Jonah muttered to the empty room, the words tasting hollow.

He crushed the cigarette into an ashtray, the ember dying with a hiss. The stash house was out there, buried in the east side's sprawl, and with it, maybe a piece of Kane's empire he could finally break. The key felt heavier now, a weight of purpose and debt. Mike had bought him this chance with his last breath Jonah owed it to him to see it through.

He stood, tucking the key and note into his pocket, his shadow long against the peeling wallpaper. The city pulsed outside, restless and rotten, but he wasn't done yet. Tomorrow, he'd chase the lead, piece together the scraps, and keep fighting. For Mike. For the truth. For whatever was left to save.

The morning broke gray and sullen, the sky a bruise over the skyline as Jonah navigated the east side's maze of warehouses and rusted piers. The docks stretched out ahead, a skeleton of industry long abandoned, cranes jutting like broken fingers against the horizon. He'd spent the night piecing together what he could from Mike's note, cross-referencing it with maps and memory, but the partial address left too many gaps. 47-something, near the water. It was a start, but a damn thin one.

He parked a block away, blending the sedan into a row of derelict vehicles, and moved on foot. The air carried salt and decay, the wind rattling loose metal and stirring trash along the cracked asphalt. His hand brushed the pistol at his hip, a reflex now, as he scanned the buildings squat, windowless hulks tagged with graffiti, their doors padlocked or boarded.

Mike's words looped in his head: *Kane's real dirt… leverage.* If the stash house held what he claimed records, tapes, proof it could be the key to dismantling what was left of Kane's network. But first, he had to find it. And not get killed in the process.

A warehouse caught his eye number 47 painted in faded white on a rusted gate, the structure half-collapsed but still standing. Too obvious, maybe, but he circled it anyway, sticking to the shadows. The gate was chained, the lock old but intact. He pulled Mike's key from his pocket, testing it. No fit. He cursed under his breath, moving on.

The next block brought more of the same warehouses and storage units, some marked with numbers in the 40s, others blank. He tried the key in every lock he found, each click of resistance tightening the knot in his gut. Time was slipping, and Kane's enforcers wouldn't be far behind. They'd known Mike talked they'd come for him, and now they'd hunt Jonah too.

He stopped at a narrow alley between two buildings, the numbers 47-09 stenciled faintly on a steel door. The key slid into the lock with a soft *snick*, turning smooth. His breath caught, adrenaline spiking. This was it.

The door creaked open, revealing a cavernous space empty save for a metal cabinet in the corner, its surface pitted with rust. Jonah crossed the room, senses on edge, the silence too loud in his ears. He tried the key again, and the cabinet unlocked, hinges groaning as he swung it wide.

Inside, a lockbox small, dented, secured with a combination. The note's smudged digits stared back at him from his pocket, useless without the full code. He slammed the cabinet shut, the clang echoing, frustration boiling over. Partial intel, just like Mike said. A lead, but not enough.

Footsteps outside quick, deliberate. Jonah ducked behind the cabinet, drawing his pistol as the door banged open. Two men, armed, swept in, their voices low and clipped. "He's here. Find him."

Jonah held his breath, finger on the trigger. The stash was close, but so were they. Another fight, another gamble. He'd come too far to lose it now.

The standoff lasted seconds, though it felt like hours. One of the men moved left, circling the room, his boots crunching glass. The other stayed near the door, weapon raised, eyes scanning the shadows. Jonah weighed his odds two against one, tight quarters, no clear exit. He'd faced worse, but not by much.

The cabinet creaked as he shifted, a faint sound but enough. The man by the door snapped his head toward it, barking, "There!" Jonah rolled out, firing as he moved. The first shot caught the door guard in the shoulder, spinning him back with a grunt. The second man lunged, but Jonah was faster, slamming him into the wall, the gun clattering free.

"Stay down," Jonah growled, pinning him with a knee. The man glared, blood trickling from a split lip, but didn't fight. The other groaned by the door, clutching his arm.

"Who sent you?" Jonah demanded, pressing the barrel to the pinned man's temple.

"Kane's people," he spat. "You're a dead man, Raines."

"Been hearing that a lot." Jonah cracked him across the jaw, knocking him out, then zip-tied both with strips from a torn jacket he found in the corner. He retrieved the lockbox, tucking it under his arm. No time to crack it here more would come.

He slipped out, the docks quiet again, the wind swallowing the echoes of the fight. The lockbox was heavy, a promise and a burden. Mike's lead had panned out, but the answers were still locked away, and the clock was ticking.

Back at the motel, Jonah worked the lockbox with a set of picks he'd scavenged years ago, the tools worn but steady in his hands. The combination eluded him hours of trial and error yielded nothing, the smudged note mocking his efforts. He leaned back, rubbing his eyes, the room's dim light blurring the edges of his vision.

Mike's face haunted him pale, bleeding, defiant to the end. "Make it mean something," he'd said. Jonah intended to. The stash house had been real, the enforcers proof it mattered. Whatever was in that box, Kane's people wanted it buried. That made it worth the risk.

He traced the note again, the partial address a puzzle he couldn't solve yet. East side, docks, 47-09 maybe a unit number, a safe code, a street crossing. Elena might know, with her knack for patterns, but reaching her meant surfacing, and the city was a net tightening around him.

A knock at the door jolted him upright, hand on his gun. He peered through the blinds nothing but shadows and the flicker of the neon sign. Paranoia, maybe, but he couldn't shake the feeling of eyes on him. Kane's machine didn't rest, and neither could he.

He packed the lockbox into a duffel, the key and note beside it. Tomorrow, he'd move, find a way to crack it, chase the next thread. The war was personal now Mike's blood, Emily's shadow, the ledger's weight. Jonah Raines was a rogue, a ghost, but he was still in the fight, and he'd drag the truth into the light no matter the cost.

The city hummed beyond the walls, a beast licking its wounds. Jonah lit another cigarette, the smoke a thin veil between him and the dark. He'd lost too much to stop now. For Mike, for the fallen, for the city rotting under Kane's shadow he'd keep going. One lead at a time.

Chapter 8: The Journalist's Edge

The safehouse was a cocoon of silence, broken only by the tapping of Elena's fingers on the keyboard and the occasional creak of the old building settling. Jonah leaned against the wall, his eyes never leaving her, his mind racing with the implications of what she was uncovering. The ledger was a Pandora's box, and every new revelation seemed to tighten the noose around their necks. Elena's silhouette stood sharp against the glow of the laptop screen as she muttered to herself, piecing together the fragments of corruption that the ledger had spilled open like blood on pavement.

Jonah admired her tenacity, the way she refused to buckle even as the shadows lengthened. But admiration was a fleeting indulgence; his focus was on keeping her alive, on ensuring Kane's reach didn't choke the life out of her. He shifted his weight, the floorboards groaning under his boots, and crossed his arms, watching as she worked.

Elena paused, her brow furrowing as she stared at the screen. "Jonah, look at this," she said, her voice a mix of excitement and dread. She pointed to a series of transactions highlighted in red. "These payments they're all routed through the same bank in the Cayman Islands. And when I trace them back, they link to shell companies tied to Vale's associates."

Jonah stepped closer, peering over her shoulder at the flickering data. "So, Vale's funneling money offshore to fund his takeover?"

"More than that," Elena said, her fingers flying over the keys as she pulled up more records. "It's a laundering operation on a massive scale. He's not just seizing Kane's network he's expanding it, using these accounts to bankroll his empire."

Jonah's jaw tightened, the familiar burn of anger flaring in his chest. "We need to verify this. If it holds, it's a kill shot."

Elena nodded, reaching for the burner phone beside her laptop. "I've got a contact who can help. Ex-SEC, now freelance. If anyone can confirm this, it's him."

She dialed, her heart thudding against her ribs as the line crackled to life. After a few rings, a gruff voice answered, "Yeah?"

"It's me," Elena said, keeping her voice low, as if the walls might betray her. "I need you to check something. Offshore accounts, Cayman Islands, tied to Marcus Vale. Can you verify?"

A pause stretched across the line, heavy with unspoken warnings. "You're digging into a viper's nest, Elena. These people don't play nice."

"I know," she replied, her grip tightening on the phone. "But I need the truth."

Another pause, longer, taut with reluctance. "Alright. Give me the details."

Elena rattled off the account numbers and transaction dates, her eyes flicking to Jonah, who watched her with a quiet intensity concern warring with pride. She could see the tension in his frame, the way his hand hovered near his pistol, always braced for the worst.

After a moment, the voice came back, clipped and urgent. "It's real. The money's flowing through shells, but it all ties back to Vale's inner circle. Watch your back, Elena. If they catch you sniffing around, they'll bury you."

"Thanks," she said, her voice steady despite the ice creeping down her spine. She hung up, setting the phone down with a hand that betrayed a faint tremor.

Jonah stepped closer, his voice a low anchor. "What'd he say?"

"It's confirmed," Elena said, meeting his gaze. "Vale's plans are bigger than we thought. He's not just consolidating he's building something unstoppable, and these accounts are the fuel."

Jonah's expression hardened, resolve carving lines into his face. "We need to stop him. Can you get more?"

Elena nodded, her mind already mapping the next steps. "I've got other sources. Risky, but they'll talk. Kane's loyalists are everywhere, though if they catch wind of this..."

"Let me handle the risk," Jonah cut in, his tone unyielding. "You get the intel. I'll keep you breathing."

Elena managed a faint smile, warmed by his stubborn protectiveness. "Together, then."

"Partners," Jonah said, a rare softness flickering in his voice.

Over the next few days, Elena threw herself into the hunt, reaching out to her web of contacts through encrypted messages and disposable phones. She met sources in the city's underbelly shadowy alleys, dive bars with sticky floors, cafes where the coffee tasted like ash always under Jonah's vigilant shadow. He stayed back, a ghost in the periphery, ensuring no one got too close as she gathered the shards of Vale's empire.

Each meeting sharpened the picture. Vale was using the offshore funds to bribe officials, secure contracts, and silence dissent. His ambition was a cancer, metastasizing with Kane's network as its host. The ledger's data wasn't just a smoking gun it was a loaded arsenal, and Elena was arming it, piece by piece.

But the deeper she dug, the louder the warnings grew. She started noticing the signs a car idling too long outside the safehouse, a figure lingering at the edge of her vision, eyes that didn't belong. She told herself it was paranoia, the weight of sleepless nights and endless coffee, but the itch wouldn't fade.

One evening, after a tense meet with a jittery whistleblower, it became real. She'd barely stepped onto the street when she felt it eyes boring into her back, sharp as knives. Her pulse spiked, and she glanced over her shoulder. A man in a dark coat trailed her, his face half-hidden by a hat pulled low, his stride too deliberate.

Elena quickened her pace, weaving through the thinning crowd, her breath shallow. She ducked into a bustling market, the air thick with the tang of fish and the chatter of vendors, hoping to shake him. But he followed, relentless, cutting through the chaos like a shark through water.

Panic clawed at her throat. She scanned for an exit, her mind racing then Jonah was there, materializing beside her like a lifeline. "Keep moving," he murmured, his arm sliding around her waist, casual but firm, as if they were just another pair in the crowd. "Don't look back."

Elena leaned into him, her fear easing under his steady presence. They threaded through the market, his touch guiding her, until they slipped into a narrow alley. He pressed her against the wall, his body shielding hers, and they waited, the world reduced to the sound of their breathing.

Footsteps echoed, then stopped. Jonah's hand tightened on his pistol, his muscles coiled. After a heartbeat that felt like an eternity, the steps retreated, swallowed by the market's din.

Elena exhaled, shaky and ragged. "That was too close."

"Way too close," Jonah said, his eyes sweeping the alley. "They're onto you. We've got to tighten up."

She nodded, gratitude flooding her chest. "Thanks, Jonah. I'd be lost without you."

He gave her a small, lopsided smile, his hand lingering on her arm. "You'd figure it out. But I'm not risking it."

Elena didn't flinch. She kept pushing, driven by a fire Jonah couldn't help but respect. Her contacts delivered documents, hushed confessions, a trail of breadcrumbs leading straight to Vale's throne. She was building a case that could topple giants, but every step forward painted a bigger target on her back.

The threats didn't let up. One night, as she pored over files in the safehouse, a brick shattered the window, glass exploding inward like a gunshot. Elena hit the floor, heart hammering, as a note skidded across the warped boards, tethered to the brick by a rubber band.

Jonah stormed in, gun drawn, his eyes wild with fury and fear. "Elena! You okay?"

She nodded, crawling to snatch the note. Her hands shook as she unfolded it: *Stop digging, or you're next.*

Jonah's face darkened, a storm brewing behind his eyes. "This stops now," he growled. "We hit back."

Elena met his gaze, her own resolve flaring. "How?"

"We find who's sending these and make them sorry," Jonah said, his voice a blade. "But first, we get you out of here."

She shook her head, fierce. "I won't run. That's what they want."

He gripped her shoulders, his stare boring into her. "You're not running. You're regrouping. We protect you so you can finish this."

Elena sighed, the logic sinking in. "Fine. But we come back harder."

"Deal," Jonah said, his tone ironclad. "Let's move."

They relocated to a new safehouse a drab apartment in a forgotten corner of the city. Jonah rigged it with cameras, alarms, anything to buy them seconds if the wolves came knocking. Elena kept at it, undeterred, her laptop a glowing lifeline in the dim space.

But the game wasn't over. Days later, she set up a meet with a source who claimed to have the keys to Vale's kingdom an insider, skittish but desperate. The rendezvous was a quiet park, the kind where kids didn't play anymore, just junkies and ghosts.

Jonah wanted to go with her, but she waved him off. "He'll bolt if he sees you. It's public he won't try anything."

He didn't like it, his gut screaming traps, but he relented. "I'll be close," he said, pointing to the ridge overlooking the park. "Signal if it goes south."

She agreed, and he watched her go, every instinct on edge.

The source was waiting on a bench, a twitchy man in a trench coat, his hands fidgeting like they wanted to run. Elena approached, her nerves humming. "You've got it?"

He nodded, sliding a USB drive across the bench. "Everything. But they're watching. Always watching."

She pocketed the drive, her fingers brushing its weight. "Thanks. Stay safe."

As she turned, two men stepped from the trees dark suits, hard eyes, Kane's dogs. They moved fast, hands twitching toward holsters. Elena's stomach dropped. She tried to sidestep, but one grabbed her arm, his grip a vice.

"Not so fast," he snarled. "You're done poking around."

Before she could twist free, Jonah's voice sliced the air. "Let her go."

He stood yards away, pistol steady, his face a mask of cold fury. The park emptied, bystanders scattering like leaves, but Jonah didn't blink, his world narrowed to the men holding Elena.

The loyalist smirked, all teeth. "Think you can take us, Raines?"

"Don't think," Jonah said, calm as death. "Know."

He fired, the shot cracking like thunder. The man gripping Elena dropped, howling, clutching his leg. The other lunged, gun flashing, but Jonah was faster kicking the weapon free, slamming him into a tree with a crunch of bone.

Elena stumbled free, gasping. "Jonah "

"Move," he barked, scanning for more. "Now."

They ran, melting into the city's arteries, the USB drive a live wire in Elena's pocket.

Back at the safehouse, Elena plugged in the drive, her hands still unsteady. The screen filled with files emails, ledgers, recordings a map of Vale's sins laid bare. "This is it," she said, voice quaking with triumph. "Everything we need to bury him."

Jonah's hand found her shoulder, solid and warm. "You're incredible, Elena. But they're not stopping."

She looked up, eyes fierce with gratitude. "I know. With you here, I can handle it."

He smiled, a crack in his armor. "We're in this together. Partners."

"Partners," she echoed, their bond a steel thread in the dark.

Elena threw herself into the endgame, weaving the evidence into a guillotine for Vale. She tapped trusted allies journalists with spines, cops not yet bought spreading the net wide and safe. Jonah turned their hideout into a fortress, traps and shadows his weapons, every move calculated to keep her alive.

Their partnership deepened, a rhythm born of necessity and trust. They read each other's silences, finished each other's plans a unit against the tide. But the threats kept coming cryptic messages, figures in the night. Jonah dealt with them, swift and brutal, a shield forged in blood.

One night, as they sifted through the latest haul, Elena paused, her gaze locking on Jonah. "I need to say this. Thank you. For everything. I'd be dead without you."

He shook his head, deflecting. "You're the one breaking this open. I'm just the muscle."

She grabbed his hand, insistent. "No. You've saved me over and over. I owe you."

"You don't owe me a damn thing," Jonah said, soft but firm. "Partners don't keep score."

Elena squeezed his hand, emotion brimming. "Then I'm damn lucky you're mine."

Jonah felt something shift, a warmth he'd buried long ago. "Same," he said, raw and honest.

In that quiet, amid the wreckage, they held onto something real a flicker of light in a city choking on its own rot. They were fighting for more than evidence now; it was justice, a shred of hope, a stand against the abyss.

The chapter closed with their partnership forged anew, a blade honed for the battles ahead. The evidence was a loaded gun, and they were ready to pull the trigger. But Kane's loyalists still prowled, and Vale's shadow loomed large. They'd won a round, but the war was just heating up.

Jonah and Elena stood together, a bulwark against the storm, their resolve a quiet roar. The city might bend, might break, but they wouldn't not yet.

Chapter 9: The Ghost

The safehouse crouched in the city's industrial underbelly, a concrete husk swallowed by shadows and the faint tang of rust. Jonah Raines sat alone at a scarred table, the ledger spread before him like a battlefield map, its inked names and numbers a litany of ghosts. The single bulb overhead flickered, casting jagged pools of light across the damp floor. His fingers brushed the page, tracing a line that ended in Mike's blood, a debt still unpaid. The air was heavy, thick with the weight of guilt and the echo of Sarah's voice, sharp with betrayal, cutting through his memory.

He leaned back, the chair groaning under him, and rubbed his face. Exhaustion clung to him like damp cloth, but sleep was a stranger. The safehouse was a relic of the city's decay abandoned warehouses and skeletal cranes loomed outside, their silhouettes stark against the bruised sky. He'd chosen it for its isolation, a place to breathe, to think, but tonight it felt like a cage. The distant hum of traffic was a taunt, a reminder of a life he'd torched to ashes.

A faint shuffle broke the silence, and Jonah's hand darted to the pistol at his hip. He turned, breath catching, and there stood Cipher silver hair glinting faintly, eyes sharp as broken glass, a figure carved from the dark. Jonah's grip eased, but his pulse didn't slow. Cipher was a phantom, slipping into his world without warning, each arrival a jolt to his frayed nerves.

"You're losing your edge, Raines," Cipher said, voice low and rough, like stones grinding together. "I could've put a bullet in you before you blinked."

Jonah snorted, holstering the gun. "Yet here I am, still breathing. What's your excuse this time?"

Cipher stepped forward, their long coat swallowing the light, and set a small encrypted drive on the table with a deliberate click. "Intel," they said. "Kane's lieutenants are meeting tomorrow night. They're scrambling to rebuild what Vale left behind. You want to hit them, this is your shot."

Jonah's chest tightened, a spark of adrenaline cutting through the fog. He picked up the drive, its weight cold in his palm, and turned it over. A meeting of Kane's remnants was a prize worth chasing, a chance to gut what was left of that empire. But Cipher's shadow loomed larger than the intel, their motives a riddle he couldn't crack. They'd pulled him from the fire before more than once but trust was a blade he'd felt too often in his back.

"Why?" Jonah asked, voice hard. "What's your angle?"

Cipher's gaze didn't waver, but their lips twitched, a flicker of something unreadable. "Kane's empire took something from me. Something I can't replace. Watching it crumble is all the reason I need."

Jonah searched their face for a lie, a crack in the mask, but found nothing. It was an answer, but not the truth not all of it. He wanted to push, to demand more, but the drive burned in his hand, a lifeline he couldn't ignore. "Where?" he said instead.

"La Sirena," Cipher replied, leaning against the wall, arms crossed. "Fancy place downtown. Private room in the back. Security's tight, but I can get you inside."

Jonah nodded, mind already spinning. La Sirena was a glittering den for the city's predators silk suits and hushed deals over wine. Kane's people meeting there was ballsy, reckless even, but that fit their pattern. He'd need Elena her tech could capture the evidence, turn their words into weapons. "Elena's in," he muttered. "She's the only one I'd trust with this."

Cipher's eyes narrowed slightly. "You sure about her?"

"More than I am about you," Jonah shot back, holding their stare.

A ghost of a smirk crossed Cipher's face. "Smart man. But trust won't be enough. You'll need a plan to walk out alive."

Jonah stood, the chair scraping loud in the stillness. "Then let's figure it out."

The map of La Sirena unfurled across the table, a tangle of lines and labels under the flickering bulb. Cipher's finger traced the service corridors, their voice steady as they laid out the terrain entrances, exits, camera blind spots. Jonah watched, unease prickling his spine. Cipher knew too much, saw too much, and every detail they offered fed the doubt gnawing at him.

"Elena goes in as a waitress," Cipher said, tapping a side entrance. "She blends in, plants the devices in the private room. You're close, inside the main floor, ready to move if it blows up. I'll hold the perimeter, pull you out if it goes bad."

Jonah frowned, picturing Elena in the crosshairs. "That's a hell of a risk for her."

"She's quick," Cipher countered, unfazed. "She'll manage. You're the one they'll spot if you're not careful."

Jonah's jaw clenched. He didn't like it Elena exposed, him playing backup, Cipher hovering like a shadow but the logic held. "And if they make her?" he pressed.

"They won't," Cipher said, voice flat. "Not if she's fast. Not if I'm watching."

He wanted to argue, to poke holes in their certainty, but the clock was ticking. "Fine," he said. "But I need more than your word. Why this meeting? Why now?"

Cipher straightened, their eyes darkening. "You think I'm setting you up?"

"I think you're holding cards I can't see," Jonah replied, stepping closer. "You always do."

For a moment, silence stretched taut between them, the air crackling with unspoken stakes. Then Cipher spoke, softer, a rare edge of something raw in their tone. "Kane's people took lives from me, same as you. That's all you need to know. We're on the same side here, Raines. For now."

Jonah held their gaze, weighing the words. It wasn't enough, but it was something a thread of shared loss he couldn't dismiss. He'd lost Mike, Carla was a question mark, and Sarah's knife still twisted in his gut. If Cipher was lying, they'd pay later. For now, the meeting was the priority.

"Alright," he said, folding the map. "We hit them tomorrow. I'll get Elena on board."

Cipher nodded, then slipped out, vanishing into the night as if they'd never been there. Jonah stood alone, the drive a cold anchor in his pocket, the ghosts of his past crowding closer.

The café was a low hum of clatter and steam, tucked on the city's fringe where no one asked questions. Jonah slid into the booth across from Elena, her laptop glowing between them, her dark hair a shield as she typed. She glanced up, sharp eyes pinning him. "You look like hell," she said, no softness in it.

"Feel like it too," Jonah replied, scanning the room habit, not paranoia. "Cipher showed up. Intel on Kane's lieutenants. They're meeting tomorrow at La Sirena."

Elena's fingers stilled, her brow creasing. "The restaurant? That's public. They're desperate."

"Or cocky," Jonah said, leaning in. "Cipher wants you undercover waitress gig, planting mics in the back room. I'll be inside, watching. They'll cover the outside."

She tapped the table, thinking fast. "Risky as hell. But if we get their plans on record, it's gold. I'm in."

Jonah exhaled, tension coiling tighter. "I don't like you in the thick of it. If they spot you "

"They won't," she cut in, firm. "I've done worse. You just keep your head down."

He nodded, trusting her steel even as his gut churned. "We pull out if it feels wrong. No chances."

"Deal," she said, a faint smile breaking through. "You're not losing me, Jonah."

Her hand brushed his, a fleeting anchor, and he gripped it briefly, the warmth a lifeline. They hashed out the details timing, signals, escape routes her mind a blade cutting through the chaos. When they parted, the city swallowed her taillights, and Jonah felt the weight of the night ahead settle like lead.

Dusk bled into the city, painting the safehouse in shades of gray. Jonah checked his pistol, the click of the slide a steady rhythm against Elena's quiet tapping as she tested the mics. The air was thick, charged, every move deliberate. Cipher arrived as the light died, a duffel bag hitting the table with a thud.

"Gear," they said, unzipping it mics, ammo, a knife Jonah didn't ask about. "You're set."

Jonah met their eyes, searching again for the lie. "This intel better be solid."

"It is," Cipher replied, unyielding. "You'll see."

Elena slipped the mics into her apron, her hands steady despite the stakes. "Ready," she said, looking to Jonah.

He nodded, throat tight. "Let's move."

The drive to La Sirena was silent, the city's glow a mocking contrast to the knot in Jonah's chest. The restaurant loomed ahead, all glass and gold, a predator's lair dressed in silk. Jonah parked a block away, watching Elena step out, her uniform a perfect mask. "Watch yourself," he said, voice low.

She flashed a tight nod and melted into the crowd. Jonah followed minutes later, slipping through a side door Cipher had marked, the noise of wealth washing over him clinking glasses, soft laughter, the reek of perfume and power.

He took a spot near the private room, blending into the edges, eyes tracking Elena as she moved graceful, invisible, a shadow among the glitter. Time dragged, each tick a hammer on his nerves. She slipped into the back room, tray steady, and Jonah held his breath as she planted the mic, her fingers a blur. She was out fast, face blank, but he saw the flicker of relief in her eyes.

Then it unraveled.

A man at the bar shifted, his stare too keen, hand brushing his coat. Another near the exit mirrored him, a bulge at his side. Jonah's blood iced they'd been clocked. He moved, shoving through the crowd as Elena's eyes met his, wide with the same realization.

"Down!" he yelled, tackling her as the first shot cracked, glass shattering. Screams erupted, chaos swallowing the room as gunmen rose, weapons flashing. Jonah fired back, dropping one, then another, his world narrowing to Elena and the exit.

They hit the kitchen, staff scattering, and burst into the alley where Cipher waited, rifle barking. "Go!" they shouted, covering as Jonah shoved Elena into the car. Bullets bit the pavement, but Cipher's aim held, and Jonah floored it, the night blurring past.

Silence fell heavy as they drove, the safehouse a sanctuary when they stumbled in. Elena sank onto a cot, shaking, and Jonah paced, fury and fear warring in his gut. Cipher followed, rifle down, face a mask.

"Someone sold us out," Jonah snapped, rounding on them. "How'd they know?"

"Not me," Cipher said, voice cold. "But we'll find out."

Elena straightened, laptop in hand. "I got the mics down. If they didn't sweep, we've got something."

They crowded the screen, audio crackling to life gruff voices plotting power, money, revenge. "Raines is a problem," one said. "But the offshore accounts come first."

Jonah's fists clenched. The accounts Elena's lead, their edge. If Kane's people got them, it was over. "We stop them," he growled. "No matter what."

Cipher nodded, resolute. "New plan. We hit back harder."

The night stretched on, the three of them bent over maps and murmurs, the ghosts of betrayal and loss hovering close. Jonah felt the war shift beneath him, a tide pulling him deeper, but with Elena's fire and Cipher's shadow, he'd face it head-on.

Chapter 10: The Ambush

The façade of La Sirena shimmered under the city's neon haze, a glittering lie draped over the corruption festering beneath. Inside, the restaurant thrummed with the pulse of wealth crystal glasses clinking, laughter spilling over polished tables, the air heavy with the mingled scents of perfume and roasted garlic. Jonah Raines sat at a corner table, his back pressed against the wall, eyes sweeping the room with the quiet intensity of a predator long accustomed to the dark. He cradled a glass of whiskey, the amber liquid untouched, a prop to mask his purpose. His gaze flicked to Elena Morales, threading her way between tables in a waitress uniform that fit her like a second skin. She was good damn good her movements smooth, her smile calibrated to charm without drawing suspicion. But Jonah caught the tightness in her shoulders, the quick dart of her eyes toward the private room's smoked-glass door, where Kane's lieutenants huddled like crows picking at a corpse.

The private room stood apart, a sanctum of heavy curtains and muted light, its entrance watched by a gorilla in a suit stretched tight across his bulk. Jonah's fingers twitched toward the pistol holstered beneath his jacket, but he kept them still, his expression a blank slate. Outside, Cipher lingered on the perimeter a shadow among shadows, their presence a cold reassurance he couldn't fully trust.

Elena slipped into the private room, tray balanced with practiced ease, and Jonah's chest tightened. She was in the heart of it now, planting the mics that could crack Kane's empire wide open. He forced his breathing to steady, willing himself to trust her nerve, but the seconds dragged like a blade across his nerves.

A murmur seeped from the private room low voices, a bark of laughter, the clink of a glass raised in a toast. Jonah strained to catch the words, but they dissolved into the restaurant's ambient hum. He checked his watch five minutes. That's all she needed. Five minutes to wire the room and get out with the evidence that could bury these bastards for good.

But time had a way of turning traitor. A man at the bar shifted, his gaze lingering on Jonah too long, his hand brushing the edge of his coat. Instinct flared, sharp and electric. Jonah scanned the room again, clocking another figure near the exit posture rigid, eyes too focused. They were made.

His hand slid to the pistol beneath the table, fingers curling around the grip. Elena emerged from the private room, her face pale but steady, and their eyes locked for a fleeting second. She gave a faint nod mics planted. Relief flickered, but it died as the man at the bar rose, his hand dipping inside his coat.

"Elena, down!" Jonah roared, surging to his feet as the first shot split the air.

The restaurant erupted screams piercing the din, glass shattering like brittle bones, the sharp tang of gunpowder flooding the space. Jonah fired back, his bullet punching through the bar gunman's chest, dropping him in a sprawl of blood and broken bottles. He lunged for Elena, yanking her behind an upturned table as rounds chewed through the wood.

"Stay low," he snapped, peering over the edge, tracking movement. The private room's door flew open, Kane's lieutenants spilling out with guns blazing. Among them, a face carved from memory Daniels, his old partner, now a snake in Kane's den.

"Raines," Daniels spat, his pistol trained on Jonah's position.

"You should've stayed in the dirt."

Anger surged, hot and bitter, but before Jonah could answer, a shot cracked from the entrance Sarah Lin, her stance steady, dropping one of Kane's men with a clean headshot. "Jonah, move!" she shouted, her voice cutting through the chaos like a lifeline.

No time to question it. Jonah grabbed Elena, hauling her toward the kitchen as Sarah laid down cover fire, her bullets stitching a path through the melee. They hit the swinging doors, but Elena faltered a meaty hand clamped onto her arm, one of Kane's goons dragging her back.

"Jonah!" Her scream was raw, her eyes wide with fear.

He wheeled, firing, but the goon used her as a shield, pressing his gun to her temple. "Drop it, Raines, or she's dead."

Jonah froze, his pistol trembling in his grip. The kitchen blurred around him stainless steel glinting, staff scattering like rats, the air thick with panic and the stench of burnt oil. Daniels advanced, his smile a twisted slash. "End of the line, Jonah. Give it up."

But Sarah materialized through the haze, silent as a wraith, her pistol rising. "Let her go, Daniels," she said, her voice ice-cold.

Daniels pivoted, shock flashing across his face. "Sarah? You're with them?"

"Always was," she replied, and squeezed the trigger.

The shot punched through Daniels' chest, blood blooming as he crumpled, his betrayal snuffed out in an instant. The goon flinched, his hold slackening, and Jonah struck lunging forward, wrenching Elena free. They bolted through the kitchen, shoving past screaming cooks, and burst into the alley where Cipher waited, engine growling.

They piled into the car, tires shrieking as Cipher floored it into the night. Jonah's pulse hammered, his mind a tangle of adrenaline and disbelief Sarah's shot, Elena's near miss, the recorder clutched in her shaking hands. They'd made it, but the weight of it clung to every ragged breath.

The safehouse crouched in a forgotten corner of the city, its peeling walls and grime-streaked windows a stark contrast to La Sirena's gloss. Inside, the air hung heavy with dust and the faint reek of mildew, but it was a refuge for now. Elena set the recorder on a scarred table, her hands unsteady as she hooked it to her laptop. The screen flared to life, casting her face in a ghostly glow, determination etched into every line.

Jonah stood by the window, staring out at the empty street, his body aching from the night's toll. Bruises throbbed along his ribs, a dull counterpoint to the storm raging in his head. Sarah lingered near the door, her posture stiff, her eyes flicking between him and the floor.

"I didn't know Daniels would be there," she said, her voice barely above a whisper. "I swear, Jonah, I didn't "

"Save it," he cut her off, sharper than he meant. He turned, the old wound of her betrayal flaring anew. "You sold me out to Vale. Don't pretend you're clean now."

She flinched, her face draining of color. "I had no choice. Vale had Carla he'd have killed her. I thought I could save you both."

Jonah's fists balled, nails biting into his palms. "You thought wrong. People died because of you Mike, Hale. How many more?"

Her eyes glistened, but she held his gaze. "I know what I did. I'll carry it forever. But I came back, Jonah. I saved you tonight. Doesn't that mean anything?"

He wanted to trust her, to let the past dull its edges, but the scars ran too deep. "It means something," he said, voice rough. "But it doesn't wipe the slate. You're here prove it. Help us end this."

She nodded, swallowing hard. "I will. Whatever it takes."

Elena's voice sliced through the tension. "Jonah, you need to hear this."

He crossed to her side, leaning over her shoulder as she hit play. The lieutenants' voices crackled through the speaker, each word a shard of ice.

"Vale's dead, but the offshore accounts are still active," one said, gruff and impatient. "We lock those down, we rebuild. Bigger than before."

Another voice slid in, oily with ambition. "The mayor's ours now. He'll sign off on whatever we need. But Raines he's a problem. Him and that journalist."

Jonah's jaw clenched, his name a venomous hiss in their mouths. Elena's hand brushed his, a quiet anchor.

"Eliminate them," a third voice said, flat and final. "No loose ends. And we need Overlord's muscle to pull it off."

The name landed like a sledgehammer. Overlord Kane's phantom enforcer, a specter Jonah had chased through blood and shadow. If he was in play, the game had just tilted hard against them.

Elena paused the audio, her eyes locking with Jonah's. "They're planning a takeover. With the mayor and Overlord, they could choke the city."

He nodded, mind racing. "We hit the accounts first. Freeze them, expose them they're crippled."

Sarah stepped closer, tentative but firm. "I can help. I've still got precinct access. Give me the numbers, and I can trace them, maybe shut them down."

Jonah studied her, weighing the gamble. Trust was a frayed thread, but desperation tipped the scales. "Do it. But one slip, Sarah, and we're through."

She gave a sharp nod, taking the account details Elena scribbled down. "I won't fail you. Not again."

As Sarah hunched over her laptop, Jonah turned to Cipher, who'd been a silent sentinel by the door. "You knew about Overlord," he said, a statement, not a question.

Cipher's eyes glinted in the dimness. "He's the key. Break him, and they fall."

Jonah's lips pressed into a thin line. "Then he's next. After the accounts."

The safehouse buzzed with fragile purpose, the team cracked but holding bracing for the fight ahead. Jonah felt the city's weight bearing down, but with Elena's resolve, Cipher's edge, and Sarah's shaky redemption, he clung to a thread of hope.

Outside, the city growled, its shadows stretching long and ravenous. But Jonah Raines stood ready, one step closer to tearing out its rotten heart.

The drive from La Sirena had been a fevered blur streetlights streaking past, the engine's roar drowning out the echoes of gunfire. Now, in the safehouse's dim stillness, the adrenaline ebbed, leaving Jonah raw and restless. He paced the cramped room, boots scuffing the worn floorboards, his mind replaying the night in jagged fragments.

Elena sat cross-legged on a sagging couch, the recorder beside her, its tiny red light a beacon in the gloom. She'd pulled her hair back, exposing the faint bruise blooming along her jaw where the goon had gripped her. She didn't flinch, didn't falter just kept working, her focus a lifeline Jonah clung to.

Sarah typed furiously at the table, her brow furrowed, fingers dancing across the keys. Every so often, she'd glance at Jonah, her expression a mix of guilt and determination. He didn't return the look couldn't, not yet.

Cipher stood apart, leaning against the wall, their silhouette stark against the peeling paint. They hadn't spoken since the alley, their silence a weight Jonah felt but couldn't decipher. Ally or liability he still wasn't sure.

The recording played again, the lieutenants' voices filling the space, each syllable a nail in Kane's coffin. Jonah listened, letting the words sink in, mapping their plans in his head. Offshore accounts, the mayor, Overlord it was a web of greed and power, and he was the fly caught in its strands.

Elena stopped the audio mid-sentence, her voice cutting through the haze. "The accounts are the linchpin. If we can't stop the money, they'll just keep coming."

Jonah nodded, rubbing the stubble along his jaw. "Sarah's on it. If she can lock them down, we buy time to hit Overlord."

"Assuming she's telling the truth," Elena said, her tone neutral but her eyes sharp.

Jonah glanced at Sarah, who paused her typing, meeting Elena's gaze. "I am," Sarah said, voice steady despite the tremor in her hands. "I've got a lead two accounts routing through a shell in the Caymans. I can freeze them, but I need a backdoor into the precinct's system."

"Do it," Jonah said, the command clipped. "We don't have room for doubt."

Sarah nodded, diving back into her work. Elena watched her for a moment longer, then turned to Jonah. "What about Overlord? If he's as big as they say "

"He is," Cipher interjected, their voice low and certain. "And he's close. Closer than you think."

Jonah's eyes narrowed. "How close?"

Cipher pushed off the wall, stepping into the light. "Close enough to know you're here. He'll come for the evidence and for you."

A chill snaked down Jonah's spine, but he masked it with a scowl. "Let him try. We'll be ready."

Elena's hand tightened on the recorder, her knuckles whitening.

"We've got the audio. That's our leverage. We just need to stay alive long enough to use it."

Jonah met her gaze, seeing the fire that had drawn him to her in the first place. "We will," he said, the words a vow. "We've come too far to lose now."

The safehouse settled into a tense rhythm Sarah's keystrokes, the hum of the laptop, the distant wail of sirens threading through the night. Jonah sank into a chair, the weight of the fight pressing down, but he didn't break. Not yet.

Hours bled into the early morning, the sky outside bruising purple. Sarah's voice broke the silence, sharp with triumph. "Got it. Accounts are frozen transfers blocked, flagged for investigation."

Jonah straightened, relief warring with exhaustion. "Good. That'll slow them down."

Elena smiled, faint but real. "One step closer."

Cipher shifted, their gaze fixed on the window. "They'll retaliate. Overlord won't wait."

"Then we don't either," Jonah said, rising. "We take the fight to him."

Sarah closed her laptop, standing to join them. "I've got precinct intel movements, patterns. It might point us to him."

Jonah studied her, the old trust flickering, fragile but there. "Alright. Let's move."

The team gathered their gear guns, the recorder, scraps of hope stitched together with grit. The city loomed beyond the door, a beast wounded but snarling, its shadows ready to swallow them whole. But Jonah Raines stepped into it, Elena at his side, Cipher a blade in the dark, Sarah a wildcard he'd play to the end.

The ambush had been a victory, but the war was just beginning. And Jonah would see it

Chapter 11: The Pawn

The safe house crouched on the edge of the city's industrial sprawl, a low-slung relic of brick and rust swallowed by the shadows of looming warehouses. Jonah Raines stood across the street, his silhouette sharp against the flickering glow of a dying streetlamp. Rain pattered against his leather jacket, a soft hiss blending with the distant rumble of traffic. He exhaled, his breath a faint cloud in the damp chill, and checked the time on his cracked watch 2:47 a.m. The night felt heavy, oppressive, like the city itself was holding its breath.

Inside, the air was thick with the stench of mold and stale smoke, the kind of place where despair settled into the cracks. Jonah's boots thudded against the worn floorboards as he moved down the narrow hall, the weight of his pistol a cold comfort against his hip. A lone guard stood outside the interrogation room, his posture rigid, eyes scanning Jonah with practiced indifference. Jonah gave a curt nod, and the guard stepped aside, the door creaking open to reveal the room beyond.

It was a box bare, utilitarian, suffocating. A steel table sat bolted to the floor, flanked by two chairs that gleamed dully under the buzzing fluorescent light. A one-way mirror stretched across the far wall, its surface a cold, unblinking eye. Carla Ramirez hunched in the chair facing him, her wrists cuffed, her dark hair spilling over her shoulders like ink. She looked diminished, fragile, a far cry from the defiant woman he'd cornered weeks ago in a back-alley deal gone sour. Now, she was a pawn, caught in Kane's web, and Jonah needed her to break free just enough to point him toward the king.

He shut the door behind him, the latch clicking like a gunshot in the silence, and crossed the room. The chair scraped as he pulled it out, the sound grating against the quiet. He sat, elbows on the table, hands clasped, and studied her. Carla didn't lift her head, her gaze locked on the scuffed surface between them, her fingers twisting in a nervous knot.

"Carla," he said, his voice low, gravelly from too many sleepless nights. "It's Jonah."

Her shoulders twitched, a flinch she couldn't hide, and her eyes darted up brief, skittish before dropping again. Fear radiated off her, sharp and raw, but beneath it was something else. Guilt, maybe. Desperation. Jonah leaned forward, the edge of the table digging into his ribs.

"I'm not here to drag you through hell," he said, softening his tone as much as he could. "You've been there already. I need your help, Carla. We're running out of time."

She shook her head, a small, frantic motion, her voice a cracked whisper. "I can't. You don't know what they'll do. My brother he's all I've got, and they'll kill him. They'll make it hurt."

Jonah's gut twisted. He'd seen Kane's playbook before leverage the weak, exploit the loyal, break them until they bent to his will. Carla wasn't a criminal by choice; she was a victim, coerced into the game by her brother's debts. He kept his face steady, masking the anger simmering beneath his skin.

"I get it," he said, his words measured. "I've had people taken from me too. Used against me. Sarah she sold me out to save her sister, and I didn't see it coming. Nearly got me killed. I know what it's like to be cornered, to feel like every move's a losing one."

Carla's eyes flicked up again, lingering this time. A spark of recognition passed between them, two souls battered by the same storm. Her lips parted, trembling, and she drew a shaky breath.

"They forced me," she said, her voice barely audible, like she was afraid the walls might hear. "My brother he owed them. Gambling, mostly, then drugs when he couldn't pay. They came to me, said I had to help or they'd... they'd cut him apart. Piece by piece."

Jonah's jaw tightened, his knuckles whitening where his hands gripped each other. Kane's cruelty was a cancer, spreading through the city, feeding on the vulnerable. He forced his voice to stay even, calm. "You're not in this alone anymore. We can keep you safe, Carla. Your brother too. But I need something from you. I need to know about Overlord."

Her head snapped up, eyes wide with terror, as if the name alone could summon him. "Overlord?" she breathed, her voice a fragile thread. "You don't you can't he's not just some thug. He's a shadow. He knows things, sees things. If I talk, he'll find out. He'll "

"Carla," Jonah cut in, firm but not harsh, leaning closer. "He's coming anyway. For you, for me, for everyone who's crossed Kane. The only way out is through him. You've got a piece of the puzzle I need it."

She stared at him, her breath shallow, her hands trembling against the cuffs. The room seemed to shrink, the air growing thick with the weight of her decision. After an eternity, she swallowed hard, her voice a whisper. "There's a warehouse. East side, near the docks. It's where they meet, where he... where Overlord shows up sometimes. I've heard him, giving orders, planning."

Jonah's pulse quickened, a jolt of adrenaline cutting through the fatigue. "Where exactly?"

She hesitated, her gaze dropping again, then forced the words out. "47-09 Harbor Street. But it's locked down tight guards, cameras, everything. If they see you…"

"I'll handle it," Jonah said, his mind already spinning with possibilities. "You've done enough."

Carla's eyes met his, pleading, desperate. "My brother promise me you'll get him out. Please, Jonah."

He reached across the table, his hand brushing hers, the cuffs clinking softly. "I'll do everything I can," he said, his voice thick with resolve. "You've got my word."

She nodded, a tear slipping free, tracing a line down her cheek. "Thank you," she murmured, barely audible.

Jonah stood, the chair scraping again, and gave her a final look a silent promise, heavy with the stakes they both understood. He turned and left, the door clicking shut behind him, sealing her back into the suffocating quiet.

The rain had picked up outside, drumming against the pavement as Jonah leaned against the safe house wall. He lit a cigarette, the flame flickering in the wet air, and took a long drag, the smoke curling into the night. Harbor Street. A lead, a real one, but it came with teeth Overlord's shadow loomed larger now, a threat he could feel in his bones. Carla's fear wasn't misplaced; if Kane's loyalists caught wind of this, the trap would snap shut fast.

His phone buzzed, cutting through the haze. He pulled it out, the screen glowing with Ramirez's name. *Meet me. Now. Usual spot.* Short, sharp, urgent. Jonah flicked the cigarette into a puddle and headed for his car, the engine growling to life as he peeled into the storm.

The diner was a dive, tucked between a shuttered pawn shop and a vacant lot, its neon sign buzzing faintly. Jonah slid into a booth near the back, the vinyl sticky under his hands, and waved off the waitress with a grunt. Ramirez slipped in minutes later, her coat dripping, her face drawn tight with exhaustion.

"You're a mess," Jonah said, pushing a mug of coffee her way.

She snorted, wrapping her hands around it. "Says the guy who looks like he hasn't slept in a week. Bureau's a circus Kane's fallout's got everyone running scared."

"What about Carla?" Jonah asked, his voice low.

"Safe, for now," Ramirez said, glancing around the empty diner. "We're moving her tonight. Can't risk a leak. What'd she give you?"

"Warehouse on Harbor Street," Jonah said, keeping his tone even. "Tied to Overlord. I'm going in."

Ramirez froze, her mug halfway to her lips. "Jonah, that's a death wish. If it's one of Kane's hubs, it's a goddamn fortress. You'll be walking into an ambush."

"Maybe," he said, meeting her gaze. "But it's a shot at Overlord. We don't get many of those."

She set the mug down hard, coffee sloshing over the rim. "You're not thinking straight. Sarah's betrayal, the hits you've taken it's pushing you too hard. Wait for me to pull a team together."

"No time," Jonah snapped, his patience fraying. "Kane's tightening his grip while we sit here talking. I'm not letting this slip."

Ramirez's eyes narrowed, frustration bleeding into her voice. "You're not a one-man army, Jonah. You've lost enough don't make me bury you too."

He leaned back, the vinyl creaking, and ran a hand over his face. "I'm not suicidal. I'm pissed. And I'm done waiting for the system to catch up."

She sighed, a sound heavy with resignation. "Fine. But if it goes south, you call me. I'll move heaven and earth to get you out."

Jonah nodded, a flicker of warmth breaking through his resolve. "Deal."

He stood, tossing cash onto the table, and stepped back into the rain, the city sprawling before him like a beast waiting to strike. Harbor Street called, a beacon or a noose he'd find out soon enough.

Back at the safe house, Jonah geared up in the dim living room, the clatter of metal sharp against the silence. Pistol loaded, knife sheathed, lockpicks tucked into his pocket. Elena paced nearby, her arms crossed, while Cipher lounged against the wall, their silver hair glinting faintly.

"You're sure?" Elena asked, her voice tight.

Jonah chambered a round, the click decisive. "It's what we've got."

Cipher pushed off the wall, their voice cool. "I'm in. You'll need eyes."

Jonah glanced at them, then nodded. "Quiet and fast. No mistakes."

Elena grabbed his arm, her grip firm. "Don't get killed, Jonah. We're not done yet."

He met her eyes, offering a half-smile that didn't reach his soul. "I'll be back."

He and Cipher slipped into the night, the rain a relentless curtain as they moved toward Harbor Street. The warehouse loomed ahead, a black monolith against the storm, its secrets buried deep. Carla had played her part, fragile and brave. Now it was Jonah's move, and the board was set for blood.

Chapter 12: The Machine

The warehouse loomed ahead, a hulking relic of the city's industrial past, its rusted steel beams and shattered windows swallowed by the night. Jonah Raines stood in the shadows across the street, his breath misting in the cold air as he scanned the perimeter. The place was a fortress of neglect, but beneath its decayed exterior, it pulsed with the lifeblood of Overlord's operations. This was no ordinary raid it was a strike at the heart of the machine that had corrupted the city, and Jonah knew the risks were higher than ever.

Cipher stood beside him, their silver hair catching the faint glow of a distant streetlamp, their eyes sharp and unreadable. They were a ghost in the dark, a blade honed by loss, and though Jonah still didn't fully trust them, he couldn't deny their skill. Cipher's intel had brought them here, to this warehouse on the edge of the docks, where Overlord's secrets lay buried like landmines.

"You sure about this?" Jonah asked, his voice low, gravelly from too many sleepless nights.

Cipher's gaze didn't waver from the warehouse. "It's solid. Overlord's been using this place to launder money and coordinate hits. The records are inside financials, hit lists, the works. We get in, grab what we need, and get out."

Jonah nodded, though doubt gnawed at him. Every lead they'd chased had come with a cost, and this one felt like a gauntlet. But they were running out of time. Kane's loyalists were regrouping, and if they didn't strike now, the machine would tighten its grip on the city.

"Let's move," Jonah said, pulling his pistol from its holster. The weight of it was a cold comfort, a reminder of the line he'd crossed from cop to rogue.

They crossed the street in silence, their footsteps muffled by the damp pavement. The warehouse's main entrance was boarded up, but Cipher led them to a side door, half-hidden behind a stack of rotting pallets. With a deft twist, they picked the lock, the door creaking open to reveal a corridor thick with dust and shadows.

Inside, the air was stale, heavy with the scent of oil and decay. Jonah's flashlight cut through the darkness, illuminating rusted machinery and crates stacked haphazardly against the walls. The place was a labyrinth, its corridors twisting like veins through the heart of the building. Every step echoed faintly, a reminder of how exposed they were.

Cipher moved ahead, their movements fluid and precise, like a predator stalking its prey. Jonah followed, his senses on high alert, every nerve attuned to the silence that felt too loud, too deliberate. They reached a stairwell, its metal steps spiraling upward into the gloom.

"Records are on the second floor," Cipher whispered, their voice barely a breath. "Security's light two guards, maybe three. We take them quietly."

Jonah nodded, his grip tightening on the pistol. They ascended the stairs, the metal groaning under their weight, each creak a potential alarm. At the top, a narrow hallway stretched before them, lined with doors that hung crooked on their hinges. Cipher pointed to the far end, where a faint light seeped from beneath a closed door.

They crept forward, Jonah's pulse thudding in his ears. As they neared the door, he heard voices low, muffled, indistinct. Cipher pressed a finger to their lips, then motioned for Jonah to take the left side. He flattened himself against the wall, his pistol raised, and waited.

Cipher kicked the door open, the wood splintering as they surged inside. Jonah followed, his weapon trained on the two guards who spun in surprise. One reached for his gun, but Cipher was faster a silenced shot dropped him before he could draw. The other raised his hands, eyes wide with fear.

"Don't," Jonah growled, his voice a low threat. "Where's the office?"

The guard's gaze flicked to a door at the back of the room, his hands trembling. "Through there," he stammered. "But it's locked. You'll need a key."

Cipher stepped forward, their pistol steady. "Give it to us."

The guard fumbled in his pocket, pulling out a ring of keys. He tossed them to Jonah, who caught them with a nod. "Stay put," Jonah said, his tone leaving no room for argument. "You move, you die."

The guard sank to his knees, hands behind his head, as Jonah and Cipher moved to the back door. Jonah slid the key into the lock, the tumblers clicking as the door swung open to reveal a small office cramped, cluttered, dominated by a desk piled high with papers and a computer humming softly in the corner.

Cipher holstered their pistol and sat at the desk, their fingers flying over the keyboard. "I'll crack the system," they said, their voice taut with focus. "You check the files."

Jonah rifled through the papers, his eyes scanning for anything that could tie Overlord to Kane's network. Financial records, transaction logs, names and dates that painted a picture of corruption so vast it made his stomach turn. But it wasn't enough he needed something concrete, something that could bring the whole machine crashing down.

"Got it," Cipher said, their voice sharp with triumph. They turned the monitor toward Jonah, revealing a list of names politicians, cops, businessmen all marked with payments and dates. And at the bottom, a hit list: Jonah Raines, Elena Morales, Cipher, and others who'd dared to challenge Kane's empire.

Jonah's blood ran cold. His name was there, stark and final, a death sentence waiting to be carried out. But it wasn't just him Elena, Cipher, even Ramirez they were all targets. The machine didn't just want them silenced; it wanted them erased.

"We need to get this out," Jonah said, his voice tight. "Copy the files, everything you can."

Cipher nodded, inserting a flash drive into the computer. The screen flickered as the data transferred, each second stretching like a taut wire. Jonah paced the small office, his mind racing. This was the evidence they needed to expose the conspiracy, to show the city how deep the rot had spread. But getting out with it was another matter.

A faint click echoed from the hallway, and Jonah froze. His hand snapped to his pistol, his senses screaming danger. "Cipher," he whispered, "we've got company."

Cipher yanked the flash drive free, their eyes meeting Jonah's with a flicker of alarm. "Go," they said, shoving the drive into their pocket. "Now."

They burst from the office, Jonah leading the way back down the corridor. But the warehouse had come alive footsteps pounded from the stairwell, voices barking orders, the clatter of weapons being readied. Kane's loyalists had found them.

Jonah's heart hammered as they sprinted through the twisting halls, the flashlight beam bouncing wildly off the walls. Behind them, the pursuit closed in, shadows stretching long and menacing. They reached the main floor, but the exit was blocked two men in tactical gear, rifles raised, their faces obscured by masks.

"Freeze!" one shouted, his voice muffled but commanding.

Jonah didn't hesitate. He fired, the shot cracking through the air, dropping one of the men as Cipher took out the other. But more were coming, their boots thundering like a storm.

"Through here," Cipher hissed, kicking open a side door that led to a loading dock. They spilled out into the night, the cold air biting at their skin, but the relief was short-lived. A black SUV screeched to a halt at the end of the alley, its doors flying open as more enforcers poured out.

Jonah and Cipher dove behind a stack of crates, bullets splintering the wood around them. The air was thick with gunfire, the sharp tang of cordite stinging Jonah's nose. He returned fire, his shots precise, but the odds were stacking against them.

"We're pinned," Cipher said, their voice steady despite the chaos. "We need a way out."

Jonah's mind raced, scanning the alley for an escape. His eyes landed on a fire escape ladder, its rusted rungs leading to the roof. "Up there," he said, nodding toward it. "We can lose them on the rooftops."

Cipher nodded, and they broke from cover, sprinting for the ladder as bullets whizzed past. Jonah reached it first, hauling himself up, his muscles straining with the effort. Cipher followed, their agility belying the danger closing in.

They reached the roof, the city sprawling below them like a jagged sea of lights and shadows. But there was no time to catch their breath. A deafening roar split the night, and the warehouse shuddered beneath them, flames erupting from the windows as an explosion tore through the building.

The shockwave knocked Jonah to his knees, the heat searing his skin even from a distance. He scrambled to his feet, grabbing Cipher's arm as they stumbled toward the edge of the roof. Below, the alley was a inferno, the SUV engulfed in flames, Kane's men scattering like rats.

"Jump!" Cipher shouted, pointing to the adjacent building, its roof a few feet lower. They leaped, landing hard on the gravel, rolling to absorb the impact. Jonah's lungs burned, his vision swimming, but he pushed himself up, dragging Cipher with him.

They ran, rooftop to rooftop, the city's skyline a blur as they put distance between themselves and the blazing warehouse. Finally, they reached a fire escape on the far side of the block, descending into a narrow alley where their car waited, hidden in the shadows.

Jonah slid behind the wheel, his hands shaking as he fumbled with the keys. Cipher collapsed into the passenger seat, clutching the flash drive like a lifeline. The engine roared to life, and they peeled out into the night, the warehouse's fiery glow fading in the rearview mirror.

Back at the safe house, Jonah paced the small room, his body thrumming with adrenaline and exhaustion. The flash drive lay on the table, its contents a ticking bomb that could either save them or damn them further. Elena sat at her laptop, her fingers flying over the keys as she decrypted the files, her face pale but resolute.

Cipher leaned against the wall, their silver hair matted with sweat, their eyes shadowed with fatigue. They hadn't spoken since the escape, their silence a weight Jonah couldn't ignore.

"You knew," Jonah said, his voice rough. "About the trap."

Cipher met his gaze, unflinching. "I didn't. But I suspected they'd have contingencies. Kane's machine doesn't die easy."

Jonah's jaw clenched, anger simmering beneath his skin. "We almost didn't make it out. If that explosion had been a second sooner "

"But it wasn't," Cipher cut in, their tone sharp. "We're alive, and we've got the evidence. That's what matters."

Jonah exhaled, forcing the tension from his shoulders. They

were right dwelling on what-ifs wouldn't change anything. The files were the key now, a glimpse into the broader conspiracy that stretched beyond Kane and Vale.

Elena's voice broke the silence, urgent and breathless. "Jonah, you need to see this."

He crossed to her side, peering over her shoulder at the screen. The files were a labyrinth of corruption bank transfers, encrypted communications, blueprints for operations that spanned the city. But one document stood out: a list of names, dates, and locations, all tied to a single codename Philip.

Jonah's brow furrowed. "Philip? Who the hell is that?"

Elena shook her head, her eyes scanning the text. "It's not a person it's a project. Look here: 'Philip Initiative Phase One: Secure funding through offshore accounts. Phase Two: Eliminate opposition.' And there's a list of targets politicians, journalists, cops. Our names are on it."

Jonah's blood ran cold. The hit list they'd found earlier was just the beginning. This was a coordinated purge, a cleansing of anyone who threatened the machine's grip on the city.

Cipher stepped forward, their expression grim. "They're not just rebuilding Kane's empire they're expanding it. This is bigger than we thought."

Jonah's mind raced, piecing together the implications. Overlord wasn't just a enforcer; he was the architect of a new order, one that would crush the city under its heel. And they were the last line of defense.

"We need to take this to Ramirez," Jonah said, his voice steady despite the storm raging inside him. "The feds can use this to dismantle the whole operation."

Elena nodded, copying the files onto a secure drive. "I'll encrypt it, make sure it's clean. But we have to be careful Kane's loyalists will be hunting us harder now."

Cipher's hand rested on their pistol, their gaze distant. "They'll come. But we'll be ready."

Jonah met their eyes, a silent understanding passing between them. They were in too deep to turn back, bound by the fight and the ghosts that drove them. The machine was vast, its gears grinding toward destruction, but Jonah Raines wasn't done yet.

He'd tear it apart, piece by piece, until the city could breathe again.

Chapter 13: The Betrayal

The rain hammered against the motel room window, a relentless drumbeat that matched the pounding in Jonah's head. He paced the small, dimly lit space, his boots scuffing against the worn carpet, his mind a storm of conflicting thoughts. Sarah sat on the edge of the bed, her hands clasped tightly in her lap, her eyes fixed on the floor. The silence between them was thick, suffocating, broken only by the occasional rumble of thunder.

Jonah stopped pacing and turned to face her, his expression a mask of barely contained anger. "You need to start talking, Sarah. Now."

She flinched at his tone, her shoulders hunching as if to ward off a blow. "Jonah, I "

"No excuses," he cut her off, his voice sharp as a blade. "You sold me out to Vale. You nearly got me killed. I want to know why."

Tears welled in her eyes, spilling over as she finally met his gaze. "I didn't have a choice," she whispered, her voice cracking. "Vale had Carla. He said he'd kill her if I didn't give him what he wanted."

Jonah's fists clenched at his sides, his knuckles white. "So you chose her over me. Over everything we've been through."

Sarah shook her head, desperation etched into every line of her face. "It wasn't like that. I tried to protect you both. I thought I could play both sides, keep you safe while saving Carla. But Vale he's ruthless. He saw through it."

Jonah's anger faltered, replaced by a hollow ache. He remembered the day they'd first met, Sarah fresh out of the academy, her eyes bright with determination. They'd been partners, friends, maybe even something more. But that was before the betrayal, before the ledger and Kane's shadow had swallowed their lives.

"You should have come to me," he said, his voice softer now, tinged with regret. "We could have figured it out together."

"I know," she said, wiping at her tears with the back of her hand. "I was scared. I didn't know who to trust. But I'm here now, Jonah. I want to make it right."

He studied her for a long moment, weighing her words against the scars of her betrayal. Finally, he sighed, rubbing a hand over his face. "Alright. Tell me what you know."

Sarah took a deep breath, steadying herself. "There's a ring of corrupt cops in the precinct. They're on Kane's payroll, covering up his operations, silencing witnesses. I can give you names, meeting spots, everything."

Jonah's eyes narrowed. "How do I know this isn't another trap?"

"You don't," she admitted, her voice trembling. "But I'm telling the truth. I swear on Carla's life."

The mention of her sister sent a pang through Jonah's chest. He knew what it was like to lose family, to have them used as leverage. Despite everything, he couldn't ignore the desperation in her eyes.

"Fine," he said, his tone grudging. "But if you're lying, Sarah, I won't hesitate to put you down."

She nodded, relief flooding her features. "I understand. Just please, help me save Carla."

Jonah turned away, his mind already racing with the implications of her intel. A corrupt cop ring was a cancer in the precinct, one that needed to be excised before it spread further. But trusting Sarah again was a gamble, one that could cost him everything.

He glanced back at her, his expression hardening. "Get some rest. We'll move on this tomorrow."

As he left the room, the rain continued to fall, a relentless reminder of the storm that still raged within him.

The stakeout was set for midnight, in a derelict part of town where the streetlights flickered like dying stars. Jonah and Cipher crouched in the shadows of an abandoned building, their eyes fixed on the precinct across the street. The building was a fortress of concrete and glass, its windows dark save for a few lights burning late into the night.

Sarah's intel had led them here, to a meeting between the corrupt cops and Kane's enforcers. If they could catch them in the act, it would be a major blow to the machine's operations.

Jonah adjusted his binoculars, scanning the entrance. "Anything?" he whispered to Cipher.

Cipher shook their head, their silver hair catching the faint light. "Not yet. But they're coming. I can feel it."

Minutes ticked by, each one stretching taut with anticipation. Then, a black SUV pulled up to the curb, its headlights cutting through the gloom. Three men stepped out, their faces obscured by the shadows, but Jonah recognized the gait of one Sergeant Mallory, a veteran cop with a reputation for brutality.

"Here they come," Jonah muttered, his grip tightening on his pistol.

The men entered the precinct, disappearing into the darkness. Jonah and Cipher waited, their breaths shallow, until the lights in a second-floor office flickered on.

"That's our cue," Cipher said, their voice a low rasp.

They slipped across the street, moving like ghosts through the night. The precinct's side door was unlocked, a testament to the arrogance of the corrupt. Jonah led the way, his boots silent on the tiled floor, his senses on high alert.

They reached the stairwell, ascending to the second floor with practiced stealth. The office door was ajar, voices drifting out a low murmur of conspiracy and greed.

Jonah peered through the crack, his heart pounding. Inside, Mallory and the enforcers huddled around a desk, stacks of cash and documents spread before them. The air was thick with the scent of cigar smoke and betrayal.

He signaled to Cipher, who nodded, their hand resting on their pistol. They burst into the room, guns raised, the element of surprise on their side.

"Freeze!" Jonah barked, his voice echoing off the walls.

The men spun, shock flashing across their faces. Mallory reached for his gun, but Cipher was faster, their shot grazing his arm, sending him stumbling back.

"Don't move," Cipher warned, their tone deadly calm.

Jonah advanced, his pistol trained on the enforcers. "Hands where I can see them. Now."

The men complied, their faces pale with fear and fury. Jonah's eyes flicked to the desk, where a ledger lay open, its pages filled with names and figures a mirror of the one that had started this nightmare.

"You've been busy," Jonah said, his voice dripping with contempt. "But it's over. We're shutting you down."

Mallory sneered, clutching his wounded arm. "You think you can stop this? Kane's machine is bigger than you know. You're just a fly in the ointment, Raines."

Jonah's jaw clenched. "Maybe. But flies can be damn annoying."

He nodded to Cipher, who began gathering the documents and

cash, stuffing them into a duffel bag. The enforcers watched, helpless, their power stripped away in an instant.

As they finished, Jonah turned to Mallory, his gaze hard. "Tell Kane we're coming for him. And when we do, there won't be a hole deep enough for him to hide in."

Mallory's face twisted with rage, but he said nothing. Jonah and Cipher backed out of the room, their guns still trained on the men, and slipped into the night.

Back at the safe house, Jonah paced the small room, his mind racing with the implications of what they'd uncovered. The corrupt cop ring was just one cog in Kane's machine, but it was a start. With the evidence they'd gathered, they could begin to dismantle the network, piece by piece.

Elena sat at her laptop, her fingers flying over the keys as she analyzed the documents. "This is gold, Jonah," she said, her voice tinged with excitement. "We've got names, dates, transactions everything we need to expose them."

Jonah nodded, but his thoughts were elsewhere. Sarah's loyalty still hung in the balance, a question mark that gnawed at him. She'd proven herself tonight, but the shadow of her betrayal loomed large.

As if sensing his turmoil, Sarah approached, her expression tentative. "Jonah, I "

"Not now," he said, holding up a hand. "We'll talk later."

She nodded, retreating to the corner of the room, her shoulders slumped.

Cipher watched the exchange, their eyes unreadable. "You still don't trust her," they said, their voice low.

Jonah sighed, rubbing his temples. "I want to. But I can't afford to be wrong again."

Cipher's gaze softened, a rare glimpse of empathy. "Trust is a luxury in this game. But sometimes, it's all we've got."

Jonah met their eyes, a silent understanding passing between them. The fight was far from over, and they needed every ally they could get even those with tarnished pasts.

As the night wore on, the team huddled around the table, plotting their next move. The corrupt cop ring was just the beginning, a thread to pull that could unravel Kane's empire. But with Sarah's loyalty in question, every step was fraught with danger.

Jonah leaned over the table, his hands braced against the scarred wood, his gaze fixed on the map spread before them. "We hit them hard and fast," he said, his voice steady despite the exhaustion creeping into his bones. "Mallory's crew is sloppy they'll crack under pressure. We use that to our advantage."

Elena looked up from her laptop, her brow furrowed. "What about the higher-ups? This ledger ties them to Kane, but we need more than names. We need proof they're calling the shots."

"That's where Sarah comes in," Cipher said, their tone neutral but their eyes flicking to her. "She's been inside. She knows how the machine works."

Sarah straightened, her hands trembling slightly as she stepped forward. "I can help. I know their routines, their weak spots. Vale used me to keep tabs on the precinct I saw things I wasn't supposed to."

Jonah's jaw tightened, his mind flashing back to the ambush that had nearly ended him. Sarah's voice had been on the other end of that call, feeding him just enough truth to lure him into Vale's trap. He forced the memory down, focusing on the present.

"Give me specifics," he said, his tone clipped. "Names, places, times. Anything we can use."

Sarah nodded, her voice gaining strength as she spoke. "There's a drop point near the docks every Thursday at 3 a.m. That's where Mallory's team meets Kane's runners. Cash for protection, no questions asked. And there's a sergeant named Haskins he's the linchpin. He reports directly to someone higher, someone Vale called 'the Broker.' I never got a name, but Haskins knows."

Jonah exchanged a glance with Cipher, who gave a slight nod. The docks were a known hotspot, a festering wound in the city's underbelly. If Sarah was telling the truth, it was a solid lead.

"Thursday's two days from now," Jonah said, his mind already mapping out the plan. "We scout it tomorrow night, get eyes on the layout. Cipher, you're with me. Elena, dig into Haskins see if his name pops in those files."

Elena's fingers resumed their dance across the keyboard. "On it."

Sarah hesitated, then spoke again. "Jonah, I can come with you. I know the signals they use, the way they move. I can spot trouble before it hits."

He turned to her, his eyes searching hers for any hint of deception. The room seemed to shrink, the air heavy with the weight of his decision. Part of him wanted to believe her, to see the Sarah he'd once trusted behind those tear-streaked eyes. But the other part the part that had felt the cold bite of betrayal screamed at him to keep her at arm's length.

"No," he said finally, his voice firm. "You stay here with Elena. We can't risk you being seen."

Her face fell, but she didn't argue, retreating back to her corner. Cipher watched her go, then leaned in close to Jonah, their voice a whisper. "You're playing it safe. Smart. But if she's legit, we might need her out there."

"I know," Jonah muttered, his gaze lingering on Sarah's slumped form. "But I'm not ready to bet our lives on 'if.'"

The planning stretched into the early hours, the team's voices a low hum against the patter of rain outside. Jonah traced routes on the map, marking entry points and escape routes, while Cipher offered terse suggestions, their mind as sharp as their aim. Elena cross-referenced Sarah's intel with the ledger, her excitement tempered by the growing list of names tied to Kane's web.

By the time the first gray light of dawn seeped through the blinds, they had a plan. It wasn't foolproof nothing in this game ever was but it was something. A chance to strike back, to turn Sarah's betrayal into a weapon against the machine that had broken her.

Jonah stepped outside, the cold air biting at his skin as he lit a cigarette. The city sprawled before him, a jagged silhouette of steel and shadow, its pulse thrumming with secrets and lies. He exhaled a plume of smoke, watching it drift into the rain-soaked morning, and wondered how many more betrayals he could endure before the weight of it all crushed him.

The next night, Jonah and Cipher moved through the docks like specters, their footsteps muffled by the damp earth and the distant groan of cranes. The air smelled of salt and rust, the water lapping against the piers in a restless rhythm. They kept to the shadows, their eyes scanning the maze of shipping containers and abandoned warehouses.

Jonah crouched behind a rusted barrel, his binoculars trained on the drop point Sarah had described a narrow alley between two warehouses, lit only by a flickering sodium lamp. Cipher knelt beside him, their silver hair tucked under a dark cap, their pistol resting lightly in their hand.

"Quiet so far," Jonah murmured, his breath fogging in the chilly air.

"Too quiet," Cipher replied, their voice a low growl. "They're either late or we're early."

Jonah checked his watch 2:45 a.m. Fifteen minutes to go. He adjusted his position, his muscles tense, his mind replaying Sarah's words. *Every Thursday at 3 a.m. Cash for protection.* If she was wrong or worse, if she'd set them up he'd know soon enough.

At 2:58, headlights pierced the darkness, a black sedan rolling slowly into the alley. Jonah's pulse quickened as two figures emerged Mallory, his arm bandaged from Cipher's bullet, and another cop Jonah didn't recognize. A third man stepped out from the shadows, a hulking figure in a leather coat, carrying a duffel bag.

"That's the runner," Cipher whispered, their eyes narrowing. "Kane's muscle."

Jonah nodded, watching as Mallory handed over a thick envelope, the exchange swift and practiced. The runner unzipped the duffel, revealing stacks of cash, and gave a curt nod. It was exactly as Sarah had said down to the signals, the timing, the way Mallory's shoulders tensed when the runner turned away.

"She wasn't lying," Jonah said, his voice barely audible. "Not about this."

Cipher's lips twitched, the closest they came to a smile. "First step. Let's see if she keeps it up."

They stayed low, documenting the meet with a small camera Elena had rigged for them. The evidence was mounting names, faces, transactions all threads in the tapestry of Kane's corruption. But Jonah knew it wasn't enough. They needed the Broker, the puppet master pulling the strings.

As the sedan pulled away and the runner melted back into the night, Jonah and Cipher retreated, their movements silent and deliberate. The docks faded behind them, swallowed by the city's endless sprawl, but the weight of what they'd seen lingered.

Back at the safe house, Jonah laid out the photos on the table, the grainy images a stark contrast to the warm glow of the single bulb overhead. Elena pored over them, cross-checking faces with her database, while Sarah hovered at the edge of the room, her eyes flicking between the pictures and Jonah.

"Haskins wasn't there," Jonah said, tapping the photo of the unknown cop. "But this guy he's new. Any hits, Elena?"

Elena shook her head, her brow creased. "Not yet. Could be a low-level grunt. I'll keep digging."

Sarah stepped closer, her voice hesitant. "That's Riggs. He's one of Haskins' guys runs errands, keeps his mouth shut. Haskins trusts him."

Jonah's gaze snapped to her, searching for any flicker of deceit. "You're sure?"

She nodded, her hands twisting together. "I saw him with Haskins once, at the precinct. Vale pointed him out said he was 'reliable.'"

Jonah filed the name away, his mind churning. Reliable or not, Riggs was a link a stepping stone to Haskins, and maybe to the Broker. He turned to Cipher, who was cleaning their pistol with methodical precision.

"We tail Riggs," Jonah said. "Find out where he goes, who he meets. If he's Haskins' errand boy, he'll lead us straight to him."

Cipher nodded, their movements pausing. "And if he doesn't?"

"Then we lean on him," Jonah replied, his tone cold. "Hard."

Sarah flinched at the words, but Jonah didn't soften them. This was the game they were playing now trust was a currency he couldn't afford to spend lightly.

Elena closed her laptop with a soft click, her eyes meeting Jonah's. "I've got a partial trace on Haskins' financials offshore accounts, small deposits. Nothing concrete, but it's a start. If Riggs ties back to him, we might have enough to force his hand."

"Good," Jonah said, his voice steady. "We keep pushing. Every piece we get brings us closer."

The room fell silent, the weight of their task settling over them like a shroud. Sarah lingered at the table's edge, her presence a quiet ache in Jonah's periphery. He wanted to trust her, to believe she'd turned a corner. But the scars of her betrayal ran deep, and every step forward felt like a tightrope walk over a chasm.

As the team dispersed Elena to her screens, Cipher to their weapons Jonah caught Sarah's eye. "You did good tonight," he said, the words grudging but sincere. "Keep it that way."

She gave a small, shaky smile, a flicker of hope in her tired eyes. "I'm trying, Jonah. I swear."

He nodded, turning away before the moment could stretch too long. The plan was set, the pieces in motion. But as he stepped into the dim hallway, the rain still drumming against the roof, he couldn't shake the feeling that Sarah's redemption and his own hung by a thread, ready to snap at the slightest misstep.

The following day, Jonah and Cipher tracked Riggs from a distance, their unmarked car blending into the city's endless flow of traffic. The man was a ghost, slipping through back alleys and dive bars, his movements erratic but purposeful. By late afternoon, they'd tailed him to a rundown gym on the edge of town a squat, brick building with peeling paint and a flickering neon sign.

Jonah parked a block away, his eyes fixed on the entrance as Riggs disappeared inside. "This could be it," he said, his voice low. "Haskins' meet spot."

Cipher cracked their knuckles, a faint smirk playing on their lips. "Only one way to find out."

They waited, the minutes dragging by, until Riggs emerged an hour later, followed by a broad-shouldered man with a buzz cut and a sergeant's swagger Haskins. Jonah's pulse kicked up a notch as he watched them exchange a few words, Haskins clapping Riggs on the shoulder before heading to a separate car.

"Bingo," Cipher muttered, already reaching for the camera.

Jonah snapped a series of shots, the click of the shutter a quiet counterpoint to the roar of his thoughts. Haskins was the key Sarah had been right again. But the question of her loyalty still gnawed at him, a splinter he couldn't dislodge.

As Haskins drove off, Jonah started the engine, his mind racing with the next steps. "We've got him," he said, his voice tight with resolve. "Now we figure out who he's reporting to."

Cipher nodded, their expression grim. "And we hope Sarah's intel holds up. One wrong move, and we're dead."

Jonah didn't reply, his eyes fixed on the road ahead. The city loomed around them, a labyrinth of light and shadow, and somewhere in its depths, the Broker waited. Whether Sarah's confession would lead them to victory or ruin, only time would tell. For now, all Jonah could do was keep moving forward, one cautious step at a time, into the heart of the betrayal that had redefined them all.

Chapter 14: The Source

The alley stretched before Jonah like a wound in the city's underbelly, its narrow confines choked with shadows and the stench of rot. Rain-slicked cobblestones gleamed under the weak glow of a single streetlamp, its light flickering as if struggling to stay alive. Jonah Raines stood at the mouth of the alley, his breath misting in the cold night air, his eyes scanning the darkness for any sign of movement. The intel had been sparse a whisper from a jittery informant, a scrap of paper with an address scrawled in haste but it was all he had. T.J. Jackson was somewhere in this labyrinth of decay, and Jonah needed him alive.

He adjusted the collar of his jacket against the chill, his fingers brushing the grip of the pistol holstered at his side. The weight of it was a familiar comfort, a reminder of the line he'd crossed from cop to rogue. But tonight, it wasn't just about survival it was about answers. T.J. was a small-time hustler, a cog in Kane's machine, but he knew things. Things that could lead Jonah to the heart of the conspiracy that had swallowed the city whole.

Jonah stepped into the alley, his boots crunching softly on broken glass. The walls loomed close, their brick faces scarred with graffiti and grime, closing in like the jaws of a trap. He moved with purpose, his senses attuned to every sound the distant wail of a siren, the skitter of rats in the shadows, the faint hum of the city beyond. Somewhere ahead, T.J. was hiding, and Jonah had to find him before Kane's enforcers did.

A flicker of movement caught his eye a shadow darting between two dumpsters, quick and furtive. Jonah's hand snapped to his pistol, but he didn't draw. Not yet. He edged forward, his heart thudding in his chest, and peered around the corner. There, crouched in the gloom, was T.J. Jackson, his wiry frame trembling, his eyes wide with fear.

"Jonah," T.J. whispered, his voice a ragged plea. "You gotta help me, man. They're coming for me."

Jonah knelt beside him, his gaze sweeping the alley for threats. "Who's coming, T.J.? Kane's people?"

T.J. nodded, his breath coming in short, panicked bursts. "Yeah. They know I've been talking. They're gonna kill me."

Jonah's jaw tightened. He'd expected this Kane's reach was long, his vengeance swift. But he hadn't anticipated how fast they'd move. "We need to get you out of here," he said, his voice low and urgent. "Now."

He grabbed T.J.'s arm, hauling him to his feet, but before they could move, the alley erupted in chaos. Gunfire split the night, bullets ricocheting off the walls, showering them with chips of brick and dust. Jonah shoved T.J. behind a dumpster, drawing his pistol in a fluid motion. His eyes locked onto the figures advancing from the alley's mouth three men, masked and armed, their movements precise and deadly.

Kane's hit squad.

Jonah fired, the shot echoing like thunder, and one of the men dropped, clutching his leg. The others scattered, taking cover behind rusted cars and overflowing trash bins. Jonah's mind raced, calculating angles and exits. They were outnumbered, outgunned, and trapped in a kill zone.

"Stay down," he barked at T.J., who huddled against the dumpster, his face pale with terror.

Jonah leaned out, squeezing off two more shots, but the enforcers were closing in, their fire relentless. A bullet grazed his shoulder, searing pain flashing through him, but he gritted his teeth and kept moving. He had to get T.J. out alive.

A narrow gap between buildings caught his eye, a sliver of escape. "This way," he hissed, grabbing T.J. and dragging him toward the opening. They squeezed through, the rough brick scraping their skin, and stumbled into an adjoining alley.

But the enforcers were relentless, their pursuit unyielding. Jonah pushed T.J. ahead, his own breath ragged, his shoulder throbbing with each step. They rounded a corner, and Jonah spotted a fire escape ladder dangling from a nearby building. It was a long shot, but it was their only chance.

"Up there," he ordered, boosting T.J. onto the ladder. The metal groaned under their weight as they climbed, the rungs slick with rain. Below, the enforcers burst into the alley, their shouts echoing off the walls.

Jonah reached the roof first, pulling T.J. up behind him. The city sprawled below them, a jagged sea of lights and shadows, indifferent to their struggle. He scanned the rooftop for an escape route, his mind racing. There a skylight, its glass cracked and filthy, leading into the building below.

He kicked it open, the glass shattering inward, and dropped through, landing hard on a concrete floor. T.J. followed, his landing less graceful, his breath coming in panicked gasps.

They were in an abandoned warehouse, its vast space filled with the skeletons of old machinery and the stench of neglect. Jonah led the way through the maze of rusted metal, his pistol at the ready, his senses straining for any sign of pursuit.

They reached a side door, and Jonah peered out into the night. The alley was clear for now. He turned to T.J., his expression hard. "We're not safe yet. You need to tell me what you know about Kane's operations. Everything."

T.J. nodded, his eyes darting nervously. "There's a server," he said, his voice trembling. "Hidden in a basement under one of

Kane's fronts. It's got everything financials, communications, dirt on everyone in the city. If you can get to it, you can bring the whole thing down."

Jonah's pulse quickened. A server that was the key, the nerve center of Kane's empire. "Where is it?"

T.J. hesitated, fear flashing in his eyes. "I I can't say. They'll kill me if they find out I told you."

Jonah grabbed him by the collar, his voice a low growl. "They're already trying to kill you. You're dead either way unless you help me stop them."

T.J. swallowed hard, his Adam's apple bobbing. "Alright. It's under the old textile factory on 5th and Harbor. But it's locked down tight guards, cameras, the works."

Jonah released him, his mind already spinning with plans. "I'll handle it. But I need you to stay hidden. Can you do that?"

T.J. nodded, relief flooding his features. "Yeah. I've got a place. Just don't let them find me."

Jonah gave a curt nod and slipped out the door, leaving T.J. to fend for himself in the shadows. The rain had lessened to a drizzle, the city's pulse thrumming around him as he made his way back to the safe house. His shoulder ached, the wound a dull throb, but he pushed it aside. There was no time for pain.

Back at the safe house, Jonah found Elena hunched over her laptop, her fingers dancing across the keys with fierce determination. The room was a cocoon of tension, the air thick with the scent of coffee and the hum of electronics. Cipher stood by the window, their silver hair catching the faint light, their eyes scanning the street below.

Jonah slumped into a chair, wincing as he peeled off his jacket. The graze on his shoulder was shallow, but it stung like hell. Elena glanced up, her brow furrowing with concern.

"You're hurt," she said, rising to grab the first aid kit.

"It's nothing," Jonah muttered, but he didn't protest as she cleaned and bandaged the wound. Her touch was gentle, a stark contrast to the violence of the night.

"What happened?" she asked, her voice soft but insistent.

"Found T.J.," Jonah said, his tone clipped. "Kane's enforcers were on him. We got out, but it was close."

Elena's eyes widened. "Did he talk?"

Jonah nodded, leaning back in the chair. "There's a server under the old textile factory on 5th and Harbor. It's got everything we need to take down Kane's operation."

Elena's breath caught, excitement flickering in her gaze. "If I can access it, I can pull the data expose the whole network."

Jonah's jaw tightened. "It's locked down tight. Guards, security systems. We'll need a plan."

Cipher turned from the window, their expression unreadable. "I can get us in. But it'll be risky."

Jonah met their gaze, a silent understanding passing between them. "We don't have a choice. This is our shot."

Elena's fingers resumed their dance across the keyboard, her mind already racing with possibilities. "I'll need to prepare get the right tools, map out the system. But if we can pull this off…"

"We will," Jonah said, his voice steady despite the exhaustion creeping into his bones. "We have to."

The safe house fell silent, the weight of their task settling over them like a shroud. Outside, the city continued its restless churn, indifferent to their struggle. But within these walls, a fragile alliance held strong, bound by a shared purpose and the ghosts of those they'd lost.

Jonah closed his eyes, the pain in his shoulder a distant echo. The server was the key, the source of Kane's power. And with Elena's skills and Cipher's edge, they'd tear it apart, piece by piece, until the machine lay in ruins.

But first, they had to survive the night.

The planning stretched into the early hours, the team huddled around the table, their voices a low murmur against the hum of the city. Elena sketched out the factory's layout on a scrap of paper, her pen moving with precision as she marked entry points and potential blind spots. Cipher offered terse suggestions, their mind a blade cutting through the chaos, while Jonah traced routes with a steady hand, his gaze fixed on the map.

By dawn, they had a plan. It wasn't perfect nothing ever was but it was a start. They'd hit the factory at midnight, when the guards changed shifts, exploiting the brief window of confusion. Elena would breach the server, downloading the data onto a portable drive, while Jonah and Cipher covered her, neutralizing any threats.

As the first light of morning seeped through the blinds, Jonah stood, stretching his stiff muscles. "Get some rest," he said, his voice rough with fatigue. "We'll need it."

Elena nodded, closing her laptop with a soft click. "I'll be ready."

Cipher lingered by the door, their expression shadowed. "We're walking into the lion's den, Raines. You sure about this?"

Jonah met their gaze, his resolve unshaken. "We don't have a choice. This is our shot to end it."

Cipher's lips twitched, a ghost of a smile. "Then let's make it count."

The safe house settled into a tense quiet, the team dispersing to their makeshift beds. Jonah lay awake, staring at the ceiling, his mind churning with the weight of what lay ahead. The server was the key, but it was also a trap, a gauntlet they had to navigate with precision and grit.

He thought of T.J., huddled in some forgotten corner of the city, his life hanging by a thread. Of Sarah, her betrayal a wound that refused to heal. Of Hale, his mentor turned traitor, his face a haunting reminder of how far the corruption had spread.

But Jonah wasn't alone. With Elena's brilliance and Cipher's steel, he had a fighting chance. And as long as he drew breath, he'd keep pushing, keep clawing at the darkness until the light broke through.

The city outside was a beast, wounded but not yet slain. Jonah closed his eyes, the rhythm of his heartbeat a steady drum against the silence. Tomorrow, they'd strike at its heart. And whatever came next, he'd face it head-on, a rogue in a war without end.

The day passed in a blur of preparation. Elena buried herself in code, her laptop a lifeline to the server's secrets, her fingers weaving a digital net to snare Kane's empire. Cipher vanished into the city, returning with a duffel bag of gear knives, flashbangs, a silenced pistol each item laid out with clinical precision. Jonah cleaned his own weapon, the familiar ritual grounding him, the metallic tang of gun oil sharp in his nose.

By nightfall, they were ready. The safe house buzzed with a quiet intensity, the air thick with unspoken stakes. Jonah pulled on his jacket, the patched shoulder stiff against his wound, and met Elena's gaze across the room.

"You good?" he asked, his voice low.

She nodded, slipping a USB drive into her pocket. "I've got the tools. Just get me to that server."

Cipher stepped forward, their silhouette a blade against the dim light. "We move fast, strike hard. No hesitation."

Jonah gave a curt nod, his hand resting on his pistol. "Let's go."

They slipped into the night, the city a maze of neon and shadow. The old textile factory loomed on the horizon, its skeletal frame a relic of a forgotten era, now a fortress guarding Kane's secrets. Jonah led the way, his steps silent on the cracked pavement, his senses sharp despite the fatigue gnawing at his edges.

They reached the perimeter, crouching behind a rusted fence. The factory's lights cast harsh pools of yellow, illuminating guards patrolling with military precision. Jonah counted five two at the gate, three roving the grounds. He glanced at Cipher, who nodded, their fingers tightening around a flashbang.

"Shift change in ten," Jonah whispered, checking his watch. "We hit then."

Elena's breath was steady beside him, her laptop clutched like a weapon. "I'll need five minutes once I'm in. Maybe less."

Jonah's eyes narrowed. "You'll get it."

The minutes ticked by, each second a hammer against his nerves. Then movement. The guards at the gate stepped aside, replaced by two fresh faces, their banter a brief lapse in discipline. Cipher moved like a shadow, lobbing the flashbang with deadly accuracy. It detonated in a blinding burst, the guards staggering, disoriented.

Jonah surged forward, pistol raised, and dropped the first guard with a single shot. Cipher took the second, their blade flashing in the dark. The roving trio spun toward the noise, weapons drawn, but Jonah and Cipher were already moving, a synchronized storm of violence. Bullets sang through the air, one clipping Jonah's sleeve, but he pressed on, his focus absolute.

They breached the factory's side entrance, Elena close behind. The interior was a cavern of dust and decay, the hum of machinery a distant pulse. Jonah led them down a stairwell, the air growing colder, heavier, until they reached a steel door reinforced, locked, a digital keypad glowing in the gloom.

"Elena," Jonah said, stepping aside.

She knelt, plugging her laptop into the keypad, her fingers a blur. "Give me ninety seconds."

Jonah and Cipher took up positions, weapons trained on the stairs. Footsteps echoed above reinforcements, drawn by the chaos outside. Jonah's pulse thudded, his shoulder aching, but he held steady.

"Got it," Elena hissed, the door clicking open.

They slipped inside, the basement a sterile contrast to the factory's ruin. The server hummed in the center, a black monolith of cables and lights. Elena plugged in, her screen flooding with data, her expression a mix of focus and triumph.

"Downloading," she said, her voice tight. "Three minutes."

Jonah nodded, turning to Cipher. "Hold the door."

Cipher's eyes gleamed. "On it."

The footsteps grew louder, shadows descending the stairs. Jonah braced himself, the weight of the night crashing down. This was it the source, the truth, the edge of the abyss. And he'd fight to the last breath to see it through.

The enforcers hit the basement like a tide, their shouts drowned by gunfire. Jonah fired from cover, each shot deliberate, each hit a step closer to survival. Cipher danced through the fray, their movements a lethal blur, bodies dropping in their wake. Blood streaked the concrete, the air thick with cordite and sweat.

"Two minutes," Elena called, her voice steady despite the chaos.

Jonah ducked a hail of bullets, his shoulder screaming as he reloaded. A guard lunged from the shadows, knife gleaming, but Jonah sidestepped, slamming the man's head into the wall. The crack of bone was a grim punctuation.

Cipher grunted, taking a hit to the arm, but they fought on, their resilience a mirror to Jonah's own. The enforcers pressed harder, their numbers thinning but their fury unrelenting. Jonah's world narrowed to the rhythm of combat aim, fire, move his mind a steel trap holding the line.

"One minute," Elena said, her fingers flying.

A grenade rolled into the room, its pin pulled. Jonah dove, kicking it back toward the stairs. The blast shook the walls, debris raining down, screams cutting through the haze. He staggered to his feet, ears ringing, and saw Cipher pinning the last guard, their knife at his throat.

"Done," Elena announced, yanking the drive free. "We've got it."

Jonah's chest heaved, adrenaline burning through him. "Move."

They bolted up the stairs, the factory a warzone of smoke and ruin. The night swallowed them as they fled, the server's secrets clutched in Elena's hand a weapon forged in blood and defiance.

Back at the safe house, the team collapsed, exhaustion a heavy shroud. Elena plugged the drive into her laptop, the screen glowing with files financials, emails, a ledger of corruption so vast it stole the breath. Jonah watched, his shoulder bandaged anew, his mind reeling at the scope of Kane's empire.

"We did it," Elena said, her voice a mix of awe and fatigue.

Jonah nodded, his gaze distant. "This is just the start."

Cipher cleaned their blade, their arm wrapped in gauze. "They'll come for us now. Harder."

"Let them," Jonah said, his voice a quiet storm. "We've got the source. And we'll use it to burn them down."

The city pulsed beyond the walls, a beast wounded but alive. Jonah leaned back, the weight of the fight settling into his bones. The war wasn't over not by a long shot. But tonight, they'd struck a blow. And that was enough for now.

Chapter 15: The Breach

The safehouse was a relic of the city's forgotten corners, a cramped basement apartment beneath a derelict tenement, its walls stained with age and the faint scent of mildew. A single bulb dangled from the ceiling, casting a weak, flickering glow over the makeshift command center Elena had assembled. Her laptop sat on a rickety table, wires snaking across the floor like veins, connecting to a tangle of external drives and routers scavenged from the black market. The air hummed with the low drone of cooling fans and the faint crackle of electricity, a symphony of tension that mirrored the knot in Jonah's stomach.

Elena Morales sat hunched over her keyboard, her fingers a blur as they danced across the keys, her face bathed in the cold blue light of the screen. Lines of code scrolled past, a language only she could decipher, her brow furrowed in concentration. Sweat beaded on her forehead despite the chill, her jaw set with a determination that Jonah had come to rely on. She was the linchpin of their operation, the one who could crack Kane's digital fortress and pull the truth from its depths. But tonight, the weight of that responsibility pressed down on her, a burden she carried with quiet resolve.

Jonah Raines paced the narrow room, his boots scuffing against the worn linoleum, his hands restless at his sides. The safehouse felt like a cage, its walls closing in with every passing second. He'd been in tighter spots before alleyway shootouts, undercover stings gone sideways but this was different. This was a battle fought in silence, in the invisible realm of ones and zeros, and it left him feeling powerless, a spectator in a war he couldn't see.

He glanced at Cipher, who stood by the boarded-up window, their silver hair catching the dim light, their eyes fixed on the street below. They were a statue of vigilance, their hand resting lightly on the pistol at their hip, their expression unreadable. Cipher had been a wildcard from the start, a ghost with motives Jonah couldn't fully trust, but their skill was undeniable. If Kane's enforcers came knocking, Cipher would be the first line of defense and the last, if it came to that.

"Anything?" Jonah asked, his voice a low rumble, rough from too many cigarettes and not enough sleep.

Elena didn't look up, her focus unbroken. "Almost there. Kane's security is military-grade layers of encryption, honeypots, the works. But I've got a backdoor. Just need to slip past the last firewall."

Jonah nodded, though the technical jargon sailed over his head. He trusted Elena's expertise, trusted her to do what he couldn't. But the waiting gnawed at him, each second a razor against his nerves. He stopped pacing and leaned against the wall, his arms crossed, his gaze flicking to the laptop screen. Lines of green text cascaded down, a waterfall of data that meant nothing to him but everything to their mission.

A soft ping broke the silence, and Elena's breath hitched. "I'm in," she whispered, her voice tinged with disbelief and triumph. "I've got access to the server."

Jonah pushed off the wall, crossing to her side in two strides. "What are we looking at?"

Elena's fingers flew over the keys, pulling up directories and files with practiced ease. "Financial records, communications logs, dossiers Kane's entire operation is here. And... wait, there's a subdirectory labeled 'Vale.' Let me see…"

She clicked, and a new window opened, revealing a trove of documents bank statements, emails, transcripts of phone calls. Jonah leaned closer, his eyes scanning the text. "What's this?"

Elena's brow furrowed as she read. "It's a paper trail linking Vale to a series of unsolved crimes murders, disappearances, all tied to Kane's rivals or whistleblowers. Look here this email from Vale to Overlord, authorizing a hit on a journalist who was getting too close."

Jonah's stomach churned, the weight of the revelation settling like lead. "Overlord's identity do we have it?"

Elena scrolled through the files, her breath quickening. "Yes. There's a file here 'Overlord Protocol.' It's encrypted, but I can crack it. Give me a minute."

She set to work, her fingers a blur, but Jonah's attention snapped to the laptop's corner, where a small alert flashed red. "Elena, what's that?"

Her eyes widened, panic flickering across her face. "Shit. They've detected the breach. They're tracing the connection."

Jonah's hand went to his pistol, his instincts screaming. "How long do we have?"

"Minutes, maybe less," Elena said, her voice tight. "I need to finish the download and wipe our tracks."

Cipher moved to the door, their pistol drawn, their stance coiled like a spring. "They'll send a team. We need to be gone before they arrive."

Jonah's mind raced, calculating their options. The safehouse was compromised they couldn't stay, but they couldn't leave without the data. "Elena, how much longer?"

"Thirty seconds," she said, her voice strained. "I'm almost there."

The seconds stretched like hours, the room thick with tension. Jonah's gaze flicked between Elena and the door, his pulse pounding in his ears. Outside, the distant wail of sirens grew louder, a harbinger of the storm closing in.

"Done," Elena breathed, yanking the USB drive from the laptop and slamming the lid shut. "We've got it."

Jonah grabbed her arm, pulling her to her feet. "We're leaving. Now."

They moved as one, Cipher leading the way, their pistol sweeping the hallway. The safehouse's back exit loomed ahead, a narrow stairwell leading up to the street. Jonah shoved the door open, the night air hitting them like a slap, cold and sharp.

But as they emerged into the alley, headlights flared at the far end, engines roaring as black SUVs screeched to a halt. Doors flew open, and Kane's enforcers spilled out, their weapons glinting in the streetlight.

"Down!" Cipher shouted, shoving Jonah and Elena behind a dumpster as gunfire erupted, bullets chewing through the brick and metal around them.

Jonah's pistol barked in response, his shots precise, dropping one enforcer as he advanced. But they were outnumbered, the alley a kill box with no clear escape. Elena crouched beside him, her laptop clutched to her chest, her eyes wide with fear.

"We're pinned," Cipher hissed, their voice steady despite the chaos. "We need to split up. Draw them off."

Jonah's gut twisted at the thought, but he knew Cipher was right. Together, they were too easy a target. "Elena, go with Cipher. I'll lead them away."

"No," Elena protested, her voice fierce. "We stay together."

"There's no time," Jonah snapped, his gaze locking with hers. "You've got the data. Get it to Ramirez. I'll meet you at the fallback point."

She hesitated, her hand gripping his arm, but Cipher was already moving, pulling her toward a side alley. "He's right. Go!"

Jonah gave her a final nod, a silent promise, and then broke cover, sprinting down the alley as bullets chased him. He fired back, his shots wild but enough to draw the enforcers' attention. Engines revved behind him, tires squealing as the SUVs gave chase.

He ducked into a narrow passage, the walls closing in, his boots pounding against the wet pavement. The city blurred around him a maze of alleys and backstreets he knew like the back of his hand. But Kane's men were relentless, their pursuit unyielding.

Jonah's breath burned in his lungs, his legs heavy with fatigue, but he pushed on, weaving through the labyrinth, losing himself in the shadows. He couldn't let them catch him not now, not with the truth so close to being exposed.

Finally, after what felt like hours, he slipped into an abandoned building, its windows boarded, its halls thick with dust. He collapsed against the wall, his chest heaving, his pistol still clenched in his hand. The sounds of pursuit faded, swallowed by the city's endless hum.

He was alone, the weight of the night pressing down on him. But he wasn't done not yet. The data was out there, in Elena's hands, a weapon to wield against Kane's empire. And as long as he drew breath, he'd keep fighting, keep clawing at the darkness until the light broke through.

For now, he'd wait, catch his breath, and plan his next move. The breach had been a victory, but the war was far from over. And Jonah Raines was ready for whatever came next.

The city sprawled beneath a sky heavy with clouds, its streets a tangle of neon and shadow, alive with the restless hum of a beast that never slept. In the safehouse, the air had been thick with the scent of stale coffee and the faint tang of solder, the detritus of their makeshift war room scattered across the floor empty cans, crumpled notes, a half-disassembled radio Elena had been tinkering with days before. Now, that sanctuary was lost, a casualty of their gambit, and Jonah felt its absence like a phantom limb.

He replayed the moment of the breach in his mind, the way Elena's hands had trembled ever so slightly as she pulled the USB drive free, the flicker of pride in her eyes before the panic set in. She'd done it cracked Kane's defenses, peeled back the layers of lies to expose the rot beneath. Vale's name tied to bodies in the morgue, Overlord's shadow stretching further than they'd dared imagine. It was the kind of evidence that could topple empires, if they could just get it into the right hands.

Cipher's voice cut through his thoughts, steady and cold as steel: *"We need to split up."* The words had landed like a punch, but they were true. Jonah had seen the math of it three of them together, weighed down by gear and desperation, were a beacon for Kane's hunters. Alone, they could slip through the cracks, become ghosts in the machine of the city.

He shifted against the wall, wincing as a bruise he hadn't noticed throbbed along his ribs. The chase had been a blur of adrenaline and instinct ducking under rusted fire escapes, vaulting over garbage-strewn crates, the echo of gunfire ringing in his ears. He'd lost count of how many corners he'd turned, how many times he'd doubled back, leading Kane's men on a wild dance through the city's underbelly. And now, here he was, holed up in a tomb of concrete and silence, waiting for the storm to pass.

Elena would be with Cipher now, moving fast, the USB drive tucked close like a heartbeat. She'd make it to Ramirez Jonah had to believe that. Ramirez, with his gruff demeanor and unshakable sense of duty, was their lifeline, the one who could turn their stolen secrets into a weapon. But the thought of Elena out there, hunted, gnawed at Jonah's resolve. She was brilliant, fierce, but she wasn't a soldier not like him, not like Cipher.

He closed his eyes, letting the cool damp of the wall seep into his back, grounding him. The city's pulse thrummed faintly through the floor, a reminder of the life beyond these walls, the stakes they were playing for. Kane's empire was a cancer, its tendrils wrapped around every institution, every street corner. The files Elena had pulled were a scalpel sharp, precise, capable of cutting deep. But a scalpel was useless if you didn't live long enough to wield it.

Jonah's grip tightened on his pistol, the metal warm from his hand. He thought of the journalist Vale had silenced, the whistleblowers vanished into the night, their stories buried under layers of concrete and corruption. That was the cost of crossing Kane, the price of truth in a city that thrived on lies. He wouldn't let Elena become another name on that list. He wouldn't let any of them.

The memory of their escape flared again the muzzle flash lighting up the alley, the acrid bite of gunpowder, the way Elena's breath had hitched as she ducked behind the dumpster. Cipher had been a shadow in motion, their shots methodical, buying them seconds that felt like borrowed time. And then the split, the wrenching moment when Jonah had turned away, drawing the fire, trusting them to make it out.

He opened his eyes, staring into the gloom. The abandoned building was a husk, its walls tagged with faded graffiti, its air thick with the must of neglect. A single window, high and cracked, let in a sliver of streetlight, painting the floor in jagged stripes. It was a temporary refuge, a pause in the chaos, but it wouldn't hold forever. Kane's men were out there, combing the streets, their resources vast and their patience thin.

Jonah pushed himself up, ignoring the ache in his legs, and checked his ammo five rounds left, enough to make a stand if it came to that. He moved to the window, peering through the gap, the city stretching out like a predator's jaws. Headlights flickered in the distance, too far to be a threat yet, but close enough to keep his nerves taut.

He wondered where Elena and Cipher were now. Had they reached the fallback point? Were they safe, or were they running too, dodging shadows and steel? The uncertainty clawed at him, but he forced it down, burying it beneath the iron of his will. They'd made a pact, the three of them Jonah, Elena, Cipher to see this through, no matter the cost. And tonight, they'd taken a step closer, struck a blow that Kane couldn't ignore.

The files were the key. Vale's crimes laid bare, Overlord's mask slipping they were cracks in the foundation, fissures that could bring the whole rotten structure down. But cracks could be patched, witnesses silenced, evidence lost. Jonah knew the game, had played it too long to believe in easy victories. This was just the beginning, a skirmish in a war that would demand everything they had.

He stepped back from the window, his boots silent on the dusty floor, and settled into a corner, his pistol resting on his knee. The city's hum filled the silence, a lullaby of danger and defiance. He'd rest here, just for a moment, let his body recover while his mind raced ahead. Then he'd move again, find Elena, find Cipher, and keep pushing forward.

The breach had been a triumph, a shard of light in the dark. But the night was long, and the shadows were deep, and Jonah Raines knew better than to trust the quiet. He'd fight on, through the alleys and the lies, until the truth was free or until it buried them all.

The alley where they'd split was a memory etched in motion now, a snapshot of chaos frozen in Jonah's mind. The dumpster's rusted edge biting into his palm as he'd braced himself, the staccato rhythm of gunfire, Elena's face pale but resolute as Cipher dragged her away. He'd seen the fear in her eyes, the unspoken question *Will I see you again?* and he'd answered it with a look, a promise he wasn't sure he could keep.

He exhaled, his breath fogging in the cold, and ran a hand through his hair, damp with sweat and grime. The chase had taken him through the city's veins past flickering streetlights, over bridges slick with rain, into the warren of backstreets where the law didn't reach. Kane's enforcers were good, trained and relentless, but Jonah was better. He'd lost them, for now, slipped through their net like smoke.

But the victory felt hollow, a fleeting reprieve. The data was out of his hands, carried by Elena into the night, and with it went their hope. He trusted her, trusted Cipher, but the weight of their separation pressed on him, a reminder of how fragile their alliance was. They were three against an army, a flicker of resistance in a city drowning in corruption.

He leaned his head back against the wall, the concrete rough against his skull, and let his thoughts drift. Elena's voice echoed in his memory, sharp and focused even as the sirens closed in: *"We've got it."* Two words, simple and heavy, carrying the weight of years years of watching Kane's empire grow, of burying friends, of chasing shadows that always slipped away. Now, they had something real, something tangible, and it terrified him as much as it thrilled him.

The USB drive held more than files it held lives, stories, the ghosts of those Kane had crushed. The journalist who'd asked too many questions, the cop who'd refused a bribe, the families left broken in the wake of Vale's orders. Jonah could feel them, a chorus of the dead urging him on, their voices mingling with the city's restless hum.

He shifted, his joints protesting, and pulled his coat tighter against the chill seeping through the walls. The abandoned building was a mausoleum, its silence a stark contrast to the chaos outside. He wondered if this was what it felt like to be a hunted man not the adrenaline of the chase, but the quiet after, the waiting, the knowing that every shadow could be a threat.

Cipher's plan had been sound split up, scatter, regroup. But it left Jonah alone with his thoughts, and that was a dangerous place to be. He thought of Sarah, her absence a wound that hadn't healed, her fate a question mark he couldn't erase. He thought of Ramirez, the grizzled fed who'd stuck his neck out for them, risking everything on a hunch that Jonah was worth believing in. And he thought of Elena, her quiet strength, her fire, the way she'd looked at him in that alley like he was her anchor.

He couldn't fail them. Not now, not when they were so close.

The distant rumble of an engine pulled him back, his senses sharpening. He eased to his feet, moving to the window again, his pistol a familiar weight in his hand. The headlights were closer now, sweeping the street below, but they didn't stop. Not yet. He watched them pass, his breath steady, his mind already mapping his next move.

The city was a battlefield, its streets a grid of danger and opportunity. Jonah knew it better than most, had walked its edges and bled on its corners. He'd find Elena, find Cipher, get the data to Ramirez. And then they'd strike again, harder, deeper, until Kane's empire was ash.

For now, he'd wait, a shadow among shadows, his resolve a blade honed by loss and purpose. The breach was done, the die cast. Whatever came next, Jonah Raines would face it head-on, a soldier in a war he couldn't afford to lose.

Chapter 16: The Hunt

The city had a way of chewing men up and spitting them out, and Jonah Raines felt every jagged tooth as he descended into its depths. The abandoned subway station was a crypt of rusted steel and shattered dreams, its platform littered with the detritus of a world that had moved on faded newspapers, broken glass, the faint hum of a city that no longer cared. He pressed himself against the damp, cracked tiles, the cold seeping through his jacket, his pistol a heavy anchor in his trembling hand. His breath came in short, ragged bursts, each one a prayer that the shadows wouldn't shift into Kane's enforcers.

Days had blurred into a relentless chase, a game of cat and mouse where Jonah was always one step from the trap. Kane's men were hounds on a scent, their pursuit unyielding, and Jonah's body bore the scars of their near misses bruises blooming across his ribs, a gash on his forearm from a knife he'd barely dodged. Sleep was a ghost, haunting him with its absence, leaving his mind a tangle of instinct and fear. He couldn't stop moving, couldn't let the exhaustion win, not when every corner held the promise of death.

The station's silence was a lie, broken by the drip of water from a leaking pipe, a sound that gnawed at his nerves like a metronome counting down to disaster. He'd chosen this place because it was a void, a forgotten artery in the city's sprawling body, but even here, he felt the weight of eyes he couldn't see.

Kane's empire was a hydra cut one head, and two more grew back and Jonah was the fool who'd dared to swing the axe.

He shifted, his boots scuffing against the grime, and a jolt of pain shot through his side. The memory of the alley fight flickered rain hammering the pavement, the enforcer's snarl, the desperate scramble over a chain-link fence. He'd gotten away, but not clean. Never clean. His free hand brushed the pistol's grip, a ritual to steady the tremor in his fingers, his gaze darting to the tunnel's black maw. Nothing moved, but the air felt thick, charged with the promise of violence.

A faint clatter echoed from the darkness, and Jonah's heart kicked hard against his chest. He raised the pistol, his body a coiled spring, every muscle screaming for release. The sound faded a rat, maybe, or the station's bones settling but it didn't matter. His mind painted threats in every shadow, every whisper of noise a prelude to the end. He forced a breath, slow and deliberate, willing his pulse to steady. He couldn't stay here. The hunt was too close, Kane's enforcers too relentless. He needed to move, to find Elena, to piece together the next step before the noose tightened.

The thought of her of Cipher, of the fragile thread tying them together kept him grounded. They'd scattered after the server breach, a calculated risk to throw Kane off their trail, but the silence since then was a blade at his throat. Had Elena made it to the fallback? Was Cipher still out there, carving a path through Kane's ranks? Jonah's jaw tightened, the uncertainty a bitter taste. They were his lifeline, the only ones who understood the stakes, and without them, he was a dead man walking.

Another sound cut through the stillness a metallic scrape, deliberate, too heavy for a rat. Jonah's breath caught, his pistol snapping up as a beam of light sliced through the tunnel's gloom. Footsteps followed, steady and purposeful, the kind that belonged to a hunter. He melted into the shadows, his back flat against the tiles, his finger hovering over the trigger. The light swept the platform, illuminating the debris in stark relief, and a figure emerged tall, lean, moving with a grace that was both familiar and deadly.

"Raines," came the voice, low and edged with steel. Cipher.

Jonah exhaled, the tension bleeding from his shoulders as he lowered the gun. Cipher stepped into the dim light, their silver hair a stark contrast to the grime, their eyes sharp and unyielding. Relief hit him like a wave, but it was fleeting Cipher's presence meant danger was closer than he'd feared.

"Thought you'd be halfway across the city by now," Jonah said, his voice rough from disuse, stepping out to meet them.

Cipher's mouth quirked, a shadow of amusement. "Had to clean up some of Kane's mess first. You're a magnet for trouble, Raines."

"Occupational hazard," Jonah muttered, holstering his pistol. "What's the situation?"

"Bad," Cipher said, their tone clipped. "Took out three of their scouts two in the warehouse district, one near the river. Bought you some breathing room, but they're swarming this sector. We need to move."

Jonah's gut twisted. "Elena?"

"With Ramirez, last I checked. She's safe, working the data. But there's more Overlord's not just a name. He's a player, high up, keeping Kane's machine running."

Jonah's eyes narrowed. "Who?"

Cipher's gaze was a blade, cutting through the haze. "Elena's got the details. We need to get to her, now. The path's clear for the moment, but it won't stay that way."

"Lead on," Jonah said, falling into step as Cipher turned back to the tunnel.

They moved fast, the flashlight's beam a lifeline in the suffocating dark. The air was heavy with damp and decay, the walls slick with condensation, every sound amplified in the claustrophobic space. Jonah's senses were razor-sharp, attuned to every drip, every scuffle, the ever-present threat of Kane's enforcers lurking just out of sight. Cipher navigated with precision, their silence a comfort and a warning they'd survived this long by being ghosts, and Jonah had to trust they'd keep him alive too.

The tunnel gave way to a service corridor, its flickering lights casting long, jagged shadows. Cipher pried open a hatch, revealing a drop into the sewers below, and Jonah followed without hesitation. The stench hit him like a fist raw sewage, rot, the city's underbelly laid bare but he swallowed the bile and pressed on, his boots splashing through the muck. The sewers were a maze, a warren of tunnels and dead ends, but Cipher moved like they'd been born to it, their steps sure and silent.

Jonah's mind churned as they went, the name *Overlord* a splinter under his skin. A high-ranking official, Cipher had said someone with power, someone who'd kept Kane's empire intact despite the cracks they'd forced into it. The ledger, the breach, the blood they'd spilled it all led to this shadow figure, and Jonah felt the weight of it pressing down, a storm building on the horizon.

A distant shout echoed through the tunnels, and Cipher froze, their hand raised in a sharp gesture. Jonah pressed against the slimy wall, his pistol drawn, his breath held as the sound of boots and voices grew louder. A patrol, moving parallel, close enough to hear but not to see. The seconds stretched, taut as a wire, until the noise faded, and Cipher signaled to move.

They picked up the pace, the air shifting as they neared the docks the tang of salt and oil cutting through the filth. The exit was ahead, a rusted grate spilling moonlight into the tunnel, but as they rounded a bend, a figure loomed an enforcer, his rifle snapping up, his face a mask of shock.

Cipher's pistol barked, a single shot that dropped him like a stone, but the sound was a thunderclap, reverberating through the sewers. "Go!" Cipher snapped, and Jonah bolted, his legs pumping as shouts erupted behind them.

The grate was a lifeline, and he scrambled through, clawing up the embankment to the docks. The night air hit him, sharp and cold, the city's skyline a jagged scar against the sky. Cipher was at his heels, firing back into the tunnel, buying seconds with every shot. "Get to Elena!" they yelled, their voice cutting through the chaos. "I'll hold them!"

Jonah hesitated, a protest on his lips, but Cipher's glare silenced him. "Move, Raines. She's got the key."

He ran, the docks a blur of steel and shadow, shipping containers rising like monoliths around him. The enforcers' cries faded, swallowed by the gunfire and the night, and Jonah pushed harder, his lungs burning, his mind locked on the fallback point. Elena was there, waiting, the truth in her hands. He couldn't fail her now.

The motel squatted on the city's edge, a crumbling relic with a flickering neon sign that buzzed like a dying insect. Jonah slipped through the back, his pistol ready, every nerve alight as he scanned the dim corridor. The room was a haze of stale smoke and desperation, and Elena sat at its heart, her laptop glowing, her face a map of worry and resolve.

"Jonah," she said, her voice breaking as she stood, crossing the space between them. "I thought "

"I'm here," he cut in, holstering his weapon, his hands finding her shoulders. "Cipher got me out. What do you have?"

She pulled back, gesturing to the screen, her eyes fierce despite the shadows beneath them. "Overlord's name. It was in the files, locked behind layers of encryption. Deputy Mayor Harlan Cross he's been running Kane's show from the top, burying evidence, shielding the whole damn operation."

The name hit Jonah like a punch, cold and hard. Cross was a fixture, a man who shook hands and smiled for the cameras while his fingers pulled every string. If he was Overlord, then Kane's empire wasn't just a criminal network it was the city itself, rotten to its core.

"We've got him," Jonah said, his voice a growl, anger coiling tight in his chest. "But he's not going down easy."

Elena nodded, her hand trembling as she pulled a flash drive from the laptop. "This has everything transactions, communications, proof he's tied to Kane and Vale. Ramirez can use it, but we need to get it to him clean."

Jonah took the drive, its weight a promise and a burden. "We will. But Kane's still out there, and Cross won't sit quiet. We need a plan."

Her fingers brushed his, a fleeting warmth in the cold. "We'll figure it out. Together."

He met her gaze, the flicker of hope in her eyes mirroring the ember in his own chest. "Together," he echoed, the word solid, a vow forged in the fire of their fight.

The hunt wasn't over Kane's enforcers were still closing in, and Cross's power loomed like a storm cloud but they had a target now, a crack in the armor. Jonah's hand tightened around the drive, his resolve hardening. The city was a beast, wounded but snarling, and they'd keep cutting until its heart stopped beating.

For now, they'd wait, plan, pray Cipher made it back. The reckoning was coming, and Jonah Raines would be ready, a soldier in a war that demanded everything he had left to give.

Chapter 17: The Confrontation

The van idled in the shadow of a crumbling overpass, its engine a low growl beneath the hiss of rain on asphalt. Jonah Raines sat in the passenger seat, his breath fogging the window as he stared at the facility across the empty lot. It was a brutalist slab of concrete and steel, squat and unremarkable, the kind of place that hid its secrets behind layers of bureaucracy and barbed wire. Floodlights carved harsh angles into the night, their glare reflecting off the puddles that dotted the cracked pavement. A chain-link fence topped with razor wire encircled the compound, a silent warning to anyone foolish enough to approach.

Jonah's hands were steady, but his heart hammered against his ribs, a relentless drumbeat of adrenaline and dread. He'd been in tight spots before alleyway shootouts, undercover ops gone sideways but this was different. This was walking into the lion's den, and the lion was waiting.

Cipher sat beside him, their silver hair catching the faint light, their eyes fixed on the facility with a predator's focus. They were a statue of calm, their fingers tapping a silent rhythm on the steering wheel, their presence both a comfort and a mystery. Jonah still didn't know what drove them, what ghosts haunted their steps, but he'd learned to trust their skill, if not their motives.

"You ready?" Cipher asked, their voice a low rasp, cutting through the tension like a blade.

Jonah nodded, his jaw tight. "Let's do this."

They slipped out of the van, the rain a cold slap against their skin, and moved toward the fence. Cipher knelt by the chain-link, pulling a pair of bolt cutters from their pack. The metal snapped with a sharp *crack*, and they peeled back a section, creating a gap just wide enough to slip through. Jonah went first, his boots sinking into the mud, his pistol a familiar weight at his hip.

The facility loomed ahead, its walls a blank face hiding a labyrinth of corridors and armed guards. Jonah's mind raced, replaying the plan they'd hammered out in the safehouse disable the cameras, bypass the patrols, find Overlord's office. It was a razor's edge, a dance with death, but they had no choice. Overlord was the key, the linchpin of Kane's empire, and tonight, they'd pull him apart.

Cipher moved like a shadow, leading them to a side entrance half-hidden by a rusted dumpster. They swiped a stolen keycard, the lock clicking open with a soft beep, and they slipped inside, the door sealing behind them with a hiss.

The corridor was sterile, fluorescent lights buzzing overhead, their harsh glow casting long shadows on the linoleum floor. Jonah's senses were on high alert, every hum and creak a potential threat. They moved quickly, Cipher's steps silent, Jonah's boots a faint scuff against the tiles. The air smelled of disinfectant and something sharper, metallic fear, maybe, or the promise of violence.

They reached a junction, and Cipher held up a hand, their eyes flicking to a security camera mounted on the ceiling. With a quick motion, they pulled a small device from their pocket a jammer, Elena had called it and pressed a button. The camera's red light blinked out, and Cipher nodded. "Clear. Thirty seconds before it resets."

They hurried down the hall, Jonah's pulse a steady thrum in his ears. The office was on the second floor, according to the blueprints, a fortified room with reinforced doors and a panic button under the desk. Overlord Deputy Mayor Harlan Cross was a man who knew how to protect himself, but tonight, his fortress would become his prison.

They climbed the stairwell, the metal steps creaking under their weight, and emerged into another corridor, this one lined with doors marked with cryptic labels *Archives, Surveillance, Interrogation*. Jonah's skin crawled, the weight of the place pressing down like a physical force. This was where Kane's machine churned, where lives were bought and sold, where the city's soul was bartered away.

Cipher stopped at a door labeled *Executive Suite*, their hand hovering over the keypad. "This is it. You ready?"

Jonah drew his pistol, the grip slick with sweat. "Do it."

Cipher punched in the code stolen from a guard's careless whisper and the door slid open with a soft hiss. They stepped inside, the office a stark contrast to the sterile halls. It was opulent, almost vulgar mahogany desk, leather chairs, a wall of monitors displaying security feeds. And behind the desk, sipping a glass of scotch, sat Harlan Cross.

He was a man carved from privilege, his silver hair slicked back, his suit tailored to perfection. His eyes were cold, calculating, the eyes of a predator who'd never known defeat. He didn't flinch as Jonah and Cipher entered, his gaze flicking over them with a mix of amusement and disdain.

"Jonah Raines," he said, his voice smooth as silk. "And the enigmatic Cipher. I've been expecting you."

Jonah's finger tightened on the trigger, but he kept the pistol steady. "Then you know why we're here."

Cross leaned back in his chair, swirling the scotch in his glass. "To take me down, I presume. To expose my 'crimes' and bring justice to the city. How quaint."

Cipher stepped forward, their voice a low growl. "You're done,

Cross. We've got the ledger, the recordings, everything. Your empire's crumbling."

Cross's smile didn't waver. "Empires don't crumble overnight, my friend. They're rebuilt, stronger than before. Kane was a visionary, but he lacked... finesse. I don't make the same mistakes."

Jonah's anger flared, a hot coal in his chest. "You're a murderer, a puppet master pulling strings while the city burns. But it ends tonight."

Cross chuckled, a sound like breaking glass. "You're a relic, Raines. A man out of time, clinging to ideals that died long ago. The city doesn't want heroes it wants order, and I provide that."

Jonah slammed his fist on the desk, the glass rattling. "Order built on blood and lies. You're going to confess, Cross. You're going to tell the world what you've done, how you're tied to Kane and Vale."

Cross's eyes narrowed, a flicker of something fear, perhaps crossing his face. "And if I refuse?"

Cipher drew their pistol, the barrel gleaming in the dim light. "We'll make you."

For a moment, silence hung heavy, the air thick with unspoken threats. Then Cross sighed, setting his glass down with a deliberate click. "Very well. If it's a confession you want, I'll give it to you. But it won't save you."

Jonah pulled a small recorder from his pocket, pressing record. "Start talking."

Cross leaned forward, his voice a venomous whisper. "I orchestrated it all the bribes, the hits, the cover-ups. Kane was the muscle, Vale the enforcer, but I was the brain. I kept the machine running, kept the city in line. And I'd do it again."

Jonah's stomach churned, the confession a bitter victory. "And the murders? The journalist, the whistleblowers who ordered those?"

"I did," Cross said, his tone flat. "They were threats to the order. Necessary sacrifices."

Cipher's hand tightened on their pistol, their knuckles white. "You're a monster."

Cross shrugged, a casual gesture that belied the weight of his words. "I'm a realist. The city needs control, and I provide it. Without me, it would descend into chaos."

Jonah shut off the recorder, his hands trembling with rage. "You're done, Cross. This goes to the feds, the press everyone. You're finished."

Cross's smile returned, sharp as a blade. "You think so? You think you've won?"

Before Jonah could respond, the door burst open, and guards flooded the room black uniforms, automatic weapons, their faces masks of cold efficiency. Jonah and Cipher spun, pistols raised, but they were outnumbered, outgunned.

"Drop your weapons," one guard barked, his rifle trained on Jonah's chest.

Jonah's mind raced, calculating the odds dismal at best. He glanced at Cipher, who gave a slight nod, their eyes flicking to the window. A desperate plan formed, a last-ditch gamble.

"Now!" Jonah shouted, diving for cover as Cipher fired, the shot shattering the window. Glass rained down, and they leaped through, landing hard on the fire escape below.

The guards opened fire, bullets chewing through the metal, but Jonah and Cipher were already moving, scrambling down the ladder, their boots slipping on the wet rungs. Alarms blared, a cacophony of sound that drowned out the pounding of their hearts.

They hit the ground running, the facility's floodlights sweeping the yard, guards pouring from every door. Jonah's lungs burned, his legs heavy with fatigue, but he pushed on, Cipher at his side, their movements a synchronized dance of survival.

A gunshot cracked, and Cipher grunted, stumbling. Jonah caught their arm, pulling them behind a stack of crates. "You hit?"

"Shoulder," Cipher hissed, their face pale but resolute. "Keep going."

Jonah peered around the crates, the guards closing in, their shouts a chorus of fury. They were trapped, the exit a gauntlet of death. He turned to Cipher, his voice tight. "We're not making it out."

Cipher's eyes met his, a flicker of something regret, perhaps, or acceptance. "Then we take as many with us as we can."

Before Jonah could reply, a new sound cut through the night sirens, loud and insistent, growing closer. Headlights flooded the lot, and vehicles screeched to a halt, their doors flying open as FBI agents spilled out, weapons drawn.

"FBI! Drop your weapons!" Ramirez's voice boomed, a lifeline in the chaos.

The guards hesitated, their rifles wavering, and in that moment, the tide turned. Agents swarmed the yard, subduing the guards, their commands sharp and unyielding. Jonah slumped against the crates, his body shaking with relief and exhaustion.

Ramirez strode toward them, his face a mask of grim determination. "You two look like hell," he said, holstering his pistol. "But you got him."

Jonah nodded, pulling the recorder from his pocket. "Confession's on here. Everything you need to bury Cross."

Ramirez took it, his grip firm. "Good work, Raines. We'll take it from here."

As the agents cuffed Cross and led him away, his face twisted with rage, Jonah felt the weight of the fight settle into his bones. It was a victory, hard-won and bitter, but it wasn't the end. Kane's machine was wounded, but it still churned, its gears grinding toward revenge.

Cipher leaned against him, their shoulder bleeding, their breath ragged. "We did it," they said, a faint smile tugging at their lips.

Jonah nodded, his gaze distant. "For now."

The rain continued to fall, a steady drumbeat against the night, washing away the blood and the grime, but not the scars. Jonah knew the war wasn't over there were still battles to fight, shadows to chase. But tonight, they'd struck a blow, and for the first time in a long while, he allowed himself to hope.

The city sprawled before him, a beast wounded but not slain, its pulse thrumming with the promise of change. Jonah Raines stood ready, a soldier in a fight that would never end, his resolve a flame that refused to die.

The aftermath was a blur of flashing lights and barked orders, the FBI agents moving with the precision of a well-oiled machine. Jonah watched from the sidelines, his body a map of bruises and exhaustion, as they secured the facility, cataloging evidence and hauling Cross's guards away in zip-ties. The rain had lessened to a drizzle, the air thick with the smell of wet concrete and gunpowder.

Cipher sat on the edge of an ambulance, a medic tending to their shoulder, their face a mask of stoic endurance. Jonah caught their eye, and they gave a slight nod, a silent acknowledgment of the hell they'd just survived. He wondered, not for the first time, what kept Cipher in this fight what debt or promise bound them to this cause. But answers were a luxury he didn't have time for, not tonight.

Ramirez approached, his trench coat soaked through, his expression a mix of relief and weariness. "Cross is singing a different tune now," he said, his voice rough from shouting.

"Trying to cut a deal, pin it all on Kane. Won't work, though not with that recording."

Jonah's lips twitched, a ghost of a smile. "Good. Let him squirm."

Ramirez clapped him on the shoulder, a rare gesture of camaraderie. "You did good, Raines. Damn reckless, but good. We've got enough here to start dismantling the network bank records, shell companies, the works."

Jonah nodded, but his eyes were fixed on the horizon, where the city's skyline loomed like a jagged scar against the night. "It's a start. But it's not enough."

"It never is," Ramirez said, following his gaze. "But it's something. Take the win, Jonah. You've earned it."

The words felt hollow, a bandage on a wound too deep to heal. Jonah turned away, his boots crunching on broken glass as he walked toward the van. The victory was real Cross in cuffs, the confession secured but it was a drop in the ocean of corruption that still drowned the city. Kane's shadow stretched long and dark, and Vale was still out there, a phantom waiting to strike.

Inside the van, he slumped into the driver's seat, the keys cold against his palm. His side ached where a guard's boot had caught him, a dull throb that matched the rhythm of his thoughts. He'd gotten what he came for, but at what cost? Another piece of himself chipped away, another night spent wading through blood and betrayal.

Cipher climbed in beside him, their movements stiff, the bandage stark white against their jacket. "You're brooding," they said, their tone dry.

Jonah snorted, a sound devoid of humor. "Just thinking."

"About?"

"Everything. Nothing." He started the engine, the rumble a low counterpoint to the silence between them. "We got him, but it doesn't feel like winning."

Cipher leaned back, their eyes half-closed. "It's not supposed to. Winning's for fairy tales. This is survival."

Jonah didn't reply, his hands tightening on the wheel. Survival. That's what it boiled down to clawing through the muck, one brutal day at a time. He pulled the van onto the road, the facility shrinking in the rearview mirror, a concrete tomb for Cross's ambitions.

The drive back was quiet, the city unfolding around them in a blur of neon and shadow. Jonah's mind churned, replaying the confrontation the smug tilt of Cross's smile, the crack of gunfire, the weight of the recorder in his hand. Each moment was a shard of glass, sharp and unyielding, cutting deeper with every breath.

He dropped Cipher at the safehouse, watching as they disappeared into the shadows, a wraith returning to its haunt. Alone now, he drove to the pier, the van's headlights slicing through the fog. The water stretched out before him, black and endless, a mirror for the void in his chest.

He killed the engine and stepped out, the wind biting through his jacket, carrying the tang of salt and decay. The city hummed behind him, a beast restless in its cage, its wounds festering beneath the surface. Cross was down, but the machine still turned gears oiled with greed and power, grinding toward its next victim.

Jonah pulled the pistol from his holster, checking the clip out of habit, the metal cold against his skin. He didn't know what came next Internal Affairs sniffing around, Elena's push to the press, the inevitable backlash from Kane's loyalists. But he knew one thing: he wasn't done. Not yet.

The confession was a weapon, a blade to cut through the rot, but it was only the beginning. He'd keep fighting, keep bleeding, until the city was free or until it buried him. There was no other path, no other choice.

He holstered the gun and leaned against the railing, the rain a soft whisper against his face. For a moment, he let himself feel it the ache, the anger, the faint flicker of hope that refused to die. It wasn't much, but it was enough.

The night stretched on, vast and unyielding, and Jonah Raines stood watch, a solitary figure against the storm.

Chapter 18: The Exposure

Elena Morales stood in the heart of the City Herald newsroom, her pulse a steady drumbeat beneath the chaos of clattering keyboards and urgent murmurs. The air was heavy with the tang of ink and stale coffee, a scent that clung to the walls like the ghosts of a thousand deadlines. She gripped the USB drive in her hand, its edges biting into her palm, a tangible anchor to the truth she'd clawed from the city's underbelly. This was no impulse it was the endgame of months spent sifting through lies, dodging Kane's enforcers, and piecing together the ledger that would unravel his empire. Her hands shook, not from fear, but from the weight of what she was about to unleash.

She crossed the room to Marcus Greene's desk, weaving through the maze of reporters hunched over screens. Marcus, the paper's grizzled watchdog, sat amidst a fortress of papers and cold mugs, his eyes sharp as broken glass. He glanced up as she approached, reading the tension in her stance like a headline.

"Elena," he rasped, voice roughened by nicotine and late nights. "You've got that look again. What's brewing?"

She didn't smile, didn't soften the edges. She handed him the drive, her fingers brushing his calloused ones. "The reckoning," she said simply.

Marcus plugged it in, his screen flickering to life with the files: the ledger names, dates, bribes in cold black and white and Overlord's confession, a recorded snarl of guilt that implicated

Kane, Vale, and half the city's power structure. His breath hitched as he scrolled, the lines on his face deepening with every revelation.

"Christ, Elena," he muttered, leaning back. "This isn't a story it's a goddamn bomb. You sure you want to light this fuse?"

"Damn sure," she said, her voice steel despite the tremor in her chest. "They've hidden long enough. The city deserves the truth."

He rubbed his jaw, eyes flicking back to the screen. "You know what's coming, right? Chaos. Resignations. Investigations. Maybe blood in the streets. And you you'll be the bullseye."

Her stomach twisted, but she held his gaze. "Let them come. I'm done running."

Marcus studied her, then gave a curt nod, a grim respect in his eyes. "Alright. Front page tomorrow. Prime real estate. But you'd better disappear after this, Morales. Kane's not the type to forgive."

She exhaled, the air sharp in her lungs. "I've been a ghost before."

The city woke to a scream of ink: **CORRUPTION EXPOSED: CITY HALL IN TURMOIL.** The *Herald* hit the stands at dawn, and by midmorning, the streets were alive with the hum of outrage. The ledger's names burned into public consciousness councilmen, cops, judges each resignation a domino toppling in a chain reaction of disgrace. The deputy mayor was first, his press conference a stammering retreat before the cameras' glare. Then the police chief, his badge surrendered under a cloud of scrutiny. By dusk, a dozen more followed, their legacies ash in the wind.

Outside city hall, the air crackled with chants and makeshift signs *Justice Now*, *Clean the Rot* as citizens pressed against barricades, their fury a living thing. News vans lined the blocks, reporters shouting over each other, their lenses trained on the unraveling spectacle. In the precincts, uniforms shifted uneasily, whispers of betrayal threading through the ranks. The investigations came swift, a swarm of subpoenas and warrants, the Feds descending like vultures on a corpse.

In a tenth-floor office, Councilman Hargrove stared at the *Herald* spread across his desk, his name circled in red. His hands shook as he poured a Scotch, the glass clinking against the bottle. He'd taken Kane's money, sure, but he'd never thought it'd come to this his career, his pension, gone in a headline. He dialed his lawyer, voice hoarse, knowing it was already too late.

Down on 12th Street, a barista named Clara paused mid-pour, the TV above the counter replaying Overlord's confession: *"Kane owned us all cops, courts, council. I just held the strings."* She felt a flicker of something hope, maybe amid the dread. For once, the city's shadows were cracking open.

But the machine wasn't dead. Kane's loyalists burrowed deeper, their silence a coiled threat. Elena watched it all from a motel room on the edge of town, the blinds slanted against the world outside. She'd struck the match, and now the fire was hers to survive.

Jonah Raines felt the knock before he heard it a dull premonition in his gut. It came at 8:00 a.m., sharp and unyielding, cutting through the drone of the TV replaying the day's chaos. He'd been awake since dawn, coffee gone cold in his mug, the apartment a wreckage of takeout boxes and unwashed clothes. The city was burning itself clean, and he was the spark that wouldn't fade.

He opened the door to two suits Internal Affairs, their badges a glint of authority under the dim hallway bulb. The taller one, Agent Pierce, spoke first, his voice a flat blade. "Detective Raines, we need a word."

Jonah stepped aside, letting them in without a fight. They took the kitchen table, him on one side, them on the other, the air thick with the scent of damp plaster and unspoken judgment.

Pierce opened a file, spreading photos and reports Elena's meetings, Jonah's off-book moves, the ledger's trail back to his hands.

"You've been busy, Raines," Pierce began, his tone clipped. "Associating with civilians, bypassing procedure, evidence that's... conveniently obtained. Care to explain?"

Jonah leaned back, arms crossed, his jaw tight. "What's to explain? I did my job. Kane's empire was choking this city cops on the take, judges in his pocket. I cut the strings."

"At what cost?" Pierce countered, sliding a photo of Jonah and Elena outside a warehouse. "You've compromised the department. Your methods unorthodox doesn't cover it. Illegal's closer."

"Illegal?" Jonah's voice rose, edged with defiance. "Kane owned half the precinct. You want to talk compromise? Look at the brass who looked the other way. I got results Overlord's singing, the ledger's out. That's what matters."

The second agent, Carter, leaned in, his eyes cold. "What matters is the chain of command. You went rogue, Raines. You think you're above the law because you're righteous?"

"I think the law failed," Jonah shot back. "Sometimes you break a few rules to fix what's broken. I'd do it again."

Pierce's gaze hardened. "That's the problem, Detective. You don't get to decide where the line is. You've put us in a bind public hero, internal liability. We're not done with you."

Jonah met his stare, unblinking. "Good. I'm not done either."

The silence stretched, a taut wire ready to snap, until Pierce closed the file with a snap. "Stay local, Raines. We'll be back."

They left, their footsteps fading down the hall, leaving Jonah with the echo of their words. He paced the cramped space, the TV flickering with images of protests and arrests. He'd known this was coming IA sniffing around, the system clawing back its control. But knowing didn't dull the sting. He'd torn open the city's wounds, and now they wanted him to bleed for it.

The rain came down in sheets as Jonah drove through the neon-streaked night, the city a blur of light and shadow. The IA grilling had left him raw, a tangle of anger and exhaustion, and he needed an anchor. Sarah had been that his sounding board, his tether through the mess of this crusade. She'd seen the dirt he'd waded through, never flinched, never judged.

But when he pulled up to her apartment, the door hung ajar, a sliver of darkness spilling out. His gut clenched as he stepped inside, the air still and heavy, her perfume a faint whisper in the emptiness. The place was gutted no couch, no books, nothing but bare walls staring back.

"Sarah?" His voice bounced off the void, unanswered.

On the counter, a note: *I'm sorry.* The ink was smudged, the words shaky, like she'd written it in a rush or a panic. Jonah's fingers tightened around it, his mind racing. Had she run, knowing the heat was coming? Or had Kane's shadow reached her first, a quiet blade in the chaos? There was no blood, no sign of struggle just absence, sharp and final.

He stood there, the note crumpling in his fist, the weight of her loss settling like damp rot in his chest. Sarah had been his constant, the one who'd kept him grounded when the lines blurred. Now she was a question mark, a hole he couldn't fill.

Jonah didn't remember driving to the pier, but there he was, the rain a steady patter against his jacket. The water stretched out, black and endless, the city's lights shivering on its surface. He lit a cigarette, the flame a brief flare against the dark, and inhaled deep, the smoke curling into the wind.

The exposure had done its work Kane's machine was fracturing, the corrupt tumbling like flies. But victory tasted like ash. Elena was in hiding, a target with a bullseye on her back. Sarah was gone, her fate a gnawing unknown. And him IA breathing down his neck, the city still teetering on a knife's edge.

He thought of the ledger, those cold columns of truth, and Overlord's voice, a cracked confession that had shattered the silence. It had been worth it, hadn't it? To rip the mask off, to let the light in? But the shadows were long, and the cost was carved into every line of his face.

The cigarette hissed as he flicked it into the water, the ember dying in the dark. The war wasn't over Kane's ghost lingered, new threats rising to fill the void. Jonah stood alone, the pier creaking beneath him, his resolve a ember still burning in the storm.

Chapter 19: The Cost

Jonah Raines stood at the edge of the pier, the city's jagged skyline a distant silhouette against the bruised sky. The wind carried the tang of salt and decay, a reminder of the city's relentless churn, indifferent to the battles fought in its shadows. He pulled his coat tighter against the chill, his hands shoved deep into his pockets, fingers brushing the worn edges of a photograph he couldn't bring himself to look at. The pier was empty, save for a few gulls picking at the remnants of the day, their cries a mournful echo in the gathering dusk.

He'd come here to think, to escape the clamor of the precinct and the endless stream of faces some grateful, others accusing that had become his daily gauntlet since the exposure. But the quiet only amplified the noise in his head, the relentless churn of memories and what-ifs that refused to settle. The victory, if it could be called that, tasted like ash. They'd torn open the city's wounds, exposed the rot, but the cost had been carved into his bones.

Lost trust. Broken bonds. A city still fractured, its wounds festering beneath a thin veneer of reform. Jonah's gaze drifted to the water, its surface rippling with the ghosts of those he'd failed Hale, his mentor turned traitor; Mike, his friend who'd sold his soul for a hospital bill; Sarah, whose absence was a wound that wouldn't heal. And Carla, caught in the crossfire, her life a bargaining chip in a game she never asked to play.

He pulled the photograph from his pocket, its edges frayed from too many nights of restless handling. It was a snapshot from a precinct barbecue, years ago Hale grinning with a beer in hand, Sarah laughing beside him, Jonah's arm slung casually over her shoulder. A moment frozen in time, before the ledger, before Kane's shadow swallowed them whole. He traced Sarah's face with his thumb, the ache in his chest a dull, persistent throb. She'd vanished without a trace, leaving only a note *I'm sorry* and the gnawing question of whether she'd run or been taken. He'd searched, of course, turned over every stone, but the city was a labyrinth of secrets, and Sarah had always been good at disappearing.

A gull landed nearby, its beady eyes fixed on him, as if waiting for an answer he didn't have. Jonah tucked the photo away, his jaw tightening. The personal toll was a ledger of its own, one he couldn't balance. He'd sacrificed everything his badge, his friendships, his peace of mind for a fight that felt like punching fog. The machine was wounded, but it still churned, its gears grinding toward the next betrayal.

Footsteps crunched on the gravel behind him, deliberate and unhurried. Jonah didn't turn, recognizing the tread Ramirez, his lifeline in the bureau, the one who'd stuck his neck out when the brass wanted Jonah buried. Ramirez stopped beside him, his trench coat flapping in the wind, his face a map of weariness and resolve.

"Thought I'd find you here," Ramirez said, his voice a low rumble. "Brooding again?"

Jonah managed a faint smile, the gesture foreign on his lips. "Just thinking."

"About?"

"Everything. Nothing." Jonah's gaze drifted back to the water. "It's a mess, Ramirez. We tore open the wound, but the infection's still there."

Ramirez nodded, his hands clasped behind his back. "It's a start.

The purge is ongoing more arrests every day. The mayor's office is scrambling, trying to distance themselves from Cross's fallout. And Carla her plea deal's solid. She's safe, Jonah. You kept your promise."

The words were a balm, but they didn't reach the ache. "She shouldn't have been in this at all. None of them should've."

Ramirez's gaze sharpened, cutting through the haze. "You did what you had to. The city's cleaner because of it. Maybe not clean, but cleaner."

Jonah's laugh was a dry, hollow sound. "Cleaner. That's a low bar."

"It's the one we've got," Ramirez said, his tone pragmatic. "You're not a martyr, Raines. You're a cop a damn good one, even if you don't wear the badge anymore. The fight's not over, but you've earned a breath."

Jonah's hands clenched in his pockets, the photograph's edges biting into his skin. "Breathing's overrated. I can't stop, Ramirez. Not while Kane's shadow still lingers."

Ramirez's expression softened, a rare crack in his armor. "I know. And you won't be alone. Elena's digging into Kane's offshore accounts new leads, new threads to pull. She's relentless, like you."

The mention of Elena stirred a flicker of warmth in Jonah's chest, a reminder that not all bonds were broken. She'd been his anchor through the storm, her fire a beacon when his own had guttered. "She's something else," he murmured, a faint smile tugging at his lips.

"She is," Ramirez agreed. "And she's waiting for you. At the diner on 5th. Said she's got something you'll want to see."

Jonah's brow furrowed, curiosity cutting through the fog. "What is it?"

Ramirez's smile was a shadow, tinged with mystery. "Go find out.

And Jonah don't forget to live a little. The fight'll still be there tomorrow."

The words hung in the air as Ramirez turned and walked away, his footsteps fading into the night. Jonah stood alone, the city's hum a distant lullaby, the pier creaking beneath him. He pulled the photograph from his pocket one last time, his thumb tracing Sarah's face, then tucked it away, a silent promise to keep searching, to keep fighting.

The diner on 5th was a relic, its neon sign buzzing sporadically, the windows fogged with steam. Jonah pushed through the door, the bell jingling faintly, and scanned the booths. Elena sat in the corner, her laptop open, her dark hair spilling over her shoulders like ink. She looked up as he approached, her eyes bright with a mix of exhaustion and triumph.

"Jonah," she said, her voice a lifeline. "You look like hell."

He slid into the booth across from her, the vinyl creaking under his weight. "Feel like it too. Ramirez said you've got something."

She nodded, turning the laptop toward him. The screen glowed with a spreadsheet bank transactions, account numbers, dates. "Kane's offshore accounts. I cracked the encryption, traced the money flow. It's a web, Jonah politicians, CEOs, even some feds. But there's a pattern, a hub where it all converges."

Jonah leaned forward, his pulse quickening. "Where?"

Elena's fingers tapped the screen, highlighting a name. "A shell company called Phoenix Holdings. It's a front, but it's tied to a physical location a warehouse on the east side. If we can hit it, we might find the next piece of the puzzle."

Jonah's mind raced, the familiar surge of purpose cutting through the fatigue. "When do we go?"

Elena's smile was a blade, sharp and ready. "Tomorrow night. But we'll need backup. Ramirez is on board, and Cipher's already scouting the area."

Jonah nodded, his resolve hardening. The fight wasn't over it never was but with Elena at his side, he felt the ember of hope flicker anew. They'd keep pushing, keep clawing at the darkness, until the city was free or they were buried beneath it.

The diner's hum faded into the background as they plotted, their voices a low murmur against the night. Jonah's gaze drifted to the window, the city's lights a constellation of promises and threats. The cost was high, the toll heavy, but he wasn't done yet. Not by a long shot.

The warehouse raid was a blur of shadows and steel, a dance of violence and precision. Jonah moved through the corridors, his pistol a steady weight in his hand, Elena at his back, her laptop clutched like a weapon. Cipher was a ghost, slipping through the guards like smoke, their blade a whisper in the dark. Ramirez's team breached the perimeter, their shouts a counterpoint to the gunfire that echoed off the walls.

They found the server room, its walls lined with humming machines, the air thick with the scent of ozone and fear. Elena plugged in, her fingers flying over the keys, her face a mask of concentration. Jonah stood guard, his senses on high alert, every nerve attuned to the chaos outside.

"Got it," Elena breathed, yanking the drive free. "Let's move."

They retreated, the warehouse a gauntlet of danger, but they made it out, the night swallowing them whole. Back at the safehouse, Elena decrypted the files, her screen filling with data financials, communications, a blueprint of corruption that stretched beyond Kane, beyond the city.

Jonah leaned over her shoulder, his breath catching as he recognized names senators, judges, CEOs a network of power and greed that dwarfed their previous victories. "This is bigger than we thought," he muttered, his voice a mix of awe and dread.

Elena nodded, her eyes fierce. "But it's a start. We'll take them down, one by one."

Jonah's hand found hers, their fingers intertwining, a silent vow forged in the fire of their fight. The cost was steep, the road ahead treacherous, but they'd walk it together, two souls bound by purpose and defiance.

The city sprawled beyond the window, a beast wounded but alive, its pulse thrumming with the promise of change. Jonah Raines stood ready, his resolve a blade honed by loss and hope, his gaze fixed on the horizon where the next battle waited.

Chapter 20: The Vigil

The pier stretched into the bay like a gnarled limb, its weathered planks groaning beneath Jonah's boots as he stood at the edge. The water lapped against the pilings, a restless murmur that mirrored the churn in his gut. A cold wind sliced through his coat, carrying the briny tang of the sea and the faint rot of the city beyond. The skyline loomed in the distance, jagged and bruised, its lights flickering like the last gasps of a dying beast. Dawn was still hours away, the sky a heavy shroud of gray, and Jonah welcomed the gloom. It suited him now, this half-light where shadows held sway.

He'd shed the badge weeks ago, left it on the precinct desk like a discarded skin, but the weight of it lingered. The city had changed since then protests swelling like a tide, voices hoarse with rage, forcing the council to bend. Arrests piled up, names he'd chased for years finally dragged into the light. Cross was gone, his empire fractured, but Jonah knew better than to call it victory. Corruption didn't die; it slithered, adapted, found new veins to poison. Kane's shadow still stretched across the bay, a specter he couldn't shake.

The photograph in his pocket pressed against his thigh, its edges worn from restless fingers. He didn't need to look at it Hale's grin, Sarah's laugh, a moment before the ledger tore it all apart. Loss was a quiet ache now, a companion he'd learned to carry, but purpose had taken root beside it. He wasn't a cop anymore, not in the way that mattered, but the fight was his. Rogue or not, he'd keep digging, keep striking at the rot until it bled out or buried him.

Gravel crunched behind him, a steady rhythm cutting through the wind. Elena. He didn't turn, just let her presence settle beside him, a warmth against the chill. She stopped at the railing, her dark hair whipping across her face, her eyes fixed on the horizon. She didn't speak at first, and he didn't need her to. They'd built something in the silence, a trust forged in blood and sleepless nights.

"Ramirez called," she said finally, her voice low, cutting through the drone of the waves. "Cipher's got eyes on a warehouse, east side. Phoenix Holdings. One of Kane's shells."

Jonah's jaw tightened, a spark igniting in his chest. "Offshore accounts?"

Elena nodded, pulling a notebook from her coat. She flipped it open, her fingers steady despite the wind. "Caymans. A web of transactions millions funneled through dummy corps. Politicians, feds, even a judge or two. It's bigger than Cross, Jonah. Kane's just the start."

He took the notebook, scanning the scrawled figures and names. The adrenaline was familiar, a jagged edge that sharpened his focus. "What's the warehouse?"

"Distribution hub," she said, her tone clipped, precise. "Records, maybe servers. If we hit it, we could crack the next layer."

Jonah handed the notebook back, his mind already racing. "Tomorrow night?"

"Ramirez is in. Cipher's scouting exits. We'll need to move fast quiet." Elena's gaze met his, steady and unyielding. "You're sure about this?"

He didn't hesitate. "I'm not stopping, Elena. Not while they're still out there."

Her lips curved, a faint, fierce smile. "Good. Neither am I."

They stood there a moment longer, the wind tugging at their coats, the city sprawling before them like a wounded giant. Public pressure had shifted it council resignations, indictments, a purge that felt like progress but Jonah saw the cracks beneath. The protests had faded, their echoes lost in the hum of traffic, but new shadows were rising, greedy hands reaching to fill Kane's void. The war wasn't won. It never would be, not fully. But he'd fight it anyway, with Elena at his side, until the end.

The diner on 5th was a ghost of its former self, its neon sign buzzing fitfully, casting a sickly glow over the cracked pavement. Jonah pushed through the door, the bell's jingle a thin, hollow sound. The air inside was thick with grease and stale coffee, the booths worn to threads. Elena sat in the corner, her laptop a faint beacon in the dimness, her hair spilling over her shoulders like spilled ink. She looked up as he approached, her eyes sharp despite the shadows beneath them.

"You look like hell," she said, her voice a lifeline in the quiet.

Jonah slid into the booth, the vinyl creaking under him. "Feel like it too. What've you got?"

She turned the laptop toward him, the screen glowing with a spreadsheet columns of numbers, dates, accounts. "Kane's offshore flow. I broke the encryption last night. It's a mess politicians, CEOs, feds. Phoenix Holdings is the hub, east side warehouse. We hit it, we get the next thread."

Jonah leaned forward, the data a map of corruption sprawling before him. Names he recognized, names he didn't, all tied to Kane's ghost. "When?"

"Tomorrow night," Elena said, her fingers tapping the table. "Ramirez has a team. Cipher's mapped the layout. We go in dark, no noise."

He nodded, the plan taking shape in his mind. "Guards?"

"Minimal. Private security, not cops. Cipher's handling recon."

Elena's gaze held his, a silent question lingering. "You're still in?"

Jonah's hand drifted to the photograph in his pocket, the weight of it grounding him. "All the way."

Her smile was a blade, quick and sure. "Then we're set."

The waitress shuffled by, refilling their coffee with a disinterested grunt, and Jonah watched the steam curl upward, dissipating into the stale air. The city outside was shifting, its pulse unsteady protests dying down, reforms inching forward but he felt the undercurrent, the quiet swell of new threats. He and Elena were rogue now, untethered from the system, but that was their strength. They'd strike from the shadows, relentless, until the next domino fell.

The warehouse loomed on the east side, a squat, rusted hulk against the night sky. Jonah crouched in the alley, his breath fogging in the chill, his pistol a cold weight in his hand. Elena was beside him, her laptop tucked into a bag slung across her chest, her face a mask of focus. Ramirez's team fanned out across the perimeter, shadows among shadows, while Cipher's voice crackled through the earpiece soft, precise, a ghost guiding them in.

"Two guards, north entrance," Cipher murmured. "Cameras offline. You've got five minutes."

Jonah nodded to Elena, and they moved, silent and swift, the gravel crunching faintly beneath their boots. The warehouse door was a slab of steel, but Cipher had already worked the lock, leaving it ajar. Inside, the air was thick with dust and the hum of machinery, a low thrum that pulsed through the walls. Rows of crates stretched into the darkness, their contents a mystery Jonah didn't have time to unravel.

Elena pointed to a stairwell, and they descended, the metal steps creaking under their weight. The server room was below, a concrete box lined with blinking machines, the air sharp with ozone. She knelt by the console, her fingers flying over the keys, while Jonah stood guard, his senses taut, every sound a potential threat.

"Got it," Elena whispered, yanking a drive from the port. "Financials, comms enough to bury them."

A shout echoed above, sharp and sudden, followed by the crack of gunfire. Ramirez's voice cut through the earpiece, clipped and urgent. "Guards tripped an alarm. We're blown."

Jonah grabbed Elena's arm, pulling her toward the exit. The warehouse erupted into chaos boots pounding, shots ringing off metal, Ramirez's team holding the line. Cipher materialized from the shadows, their blade a blur as they took down a guard rushing the stairs. The four of them fought their way out, a brutal ballet of steel and will, the night swallowing them as they broke free.

Back at the safehouse, Elena decrypted the files, her screen a cascade of data names, dates, a network of greed that stretched beyond Kane, beyond the city. Jonah stood over her shoulder, his breath catching as he recognized the scope senators, judges, a web of power that dwarfed their earlier wins.

"This is bigger than we thought," he muttered, dread and resolve warring in his chest.

Elena's eyes were fierce, unyielding. "But it's a start. We'll take them down, one by one."

Her hand found his, their fingers locking, a vow etched in the silence. The city beyond the window was a beast stirring, its wounds raw but its pulse alive. They'd keep fighting, together, until it was free or until it claimed them.

The pier was empty now, the wind sharper, carrying the promise of rain. Jonah stood alone, the city's lights flickering across the water like scattered embers. The protests had faded, their fury spent, but the air held a new tension, a quiet before the next storm. Kane's empire was cracked, its pieces scattered, yet the shadows were shifting, new players rising to claim the ruins.

He pulled the photograph from his pocket, its edges soft with wear, and traced Sarah's face one last time before tucking it away. Loss had shaped him, hollowed him, but it had also forged him tempered his resolve into something unyielding. He wasn't a hero, never had been. Just a man who couldn't look away, who'd keep standing against the tide no matter the cost.

The horizon was a thin line, dark and endless, and Jonah watched it, his stance steady, his eyes clear. The war wasn't over. It never would be. But he was ready for the next lead, the next fight, the next shadow to step into the light. The city teetered on the edge of change, and Jonah Raines stood at its brink, a solitary figure honed by loss and purpose, waiting for whatever came next.

Epilogue

The city stretched out below the pier, its skyline a jagged silhouette against the bruised dusk. Jonah Raines stood at the edge, his silhouette a solitary figure against the fading light, the wind tugging at his coat like a restless ghost. The water lapped against the pilings, a rhythmic murmur that echoed the city's restless heartbeat. Protests had ebbed, their fervor swallowed by the relentless grind of daily life, but the air still crackled with an undercurrent of change a fragile hope tempered by the shadows that clung to every corner.

Jonah's gaze swept the horizon, where the lights of the city flickered like distant stars, each one a promise and a lie. Kane's empire was fractured, its remnants scattered, but new threats loomed in the periphery, eager to claim the void. He knew this war was far from won; it was a battle fought in increments, each victory a step toward a horizon that always seemed just out of reach.

His hand slipped into his pocket, fingers brushing the worn edges of the photograph Hale, Sarah, a moment frozen in time. The ache of their absence was a constant companion, a reminder of the cost he'd paid. Yet, in the quiet of the pier, with the city sprawling before him, Jonah felt a flicker of resolve, tempered by loss but unyielding. He was no longer a cop, no longer bound by the badge, but the fight was his a vigil he'd sworn to keep, for the city, for the fallen, for himself.

The wind carried the distant hum of traffic, the faint wail of a siren, the pulse of a city teetering on the edge. Jonah turned away from the water, his boots steady on the weathered planks, his eyes fixed on the skyline. The next threat waited in the shadows, but he was ready alone, perhaps, but unbroken, his purpose a blade honed by sacrifice and hope.

Epilogue: Ashes in the Code

T he city bled neon into the puddles, the rain a steady hiss against the cracked pavement. Somewhere, deep beneath the streets Jonah Raines once patrolled, the forgotten servers hummed relics of an older system no one admitted still existed.

In a rusting data center near the river, a terminal flickered awake. No hands touched it. No operator gave the command. It simply woke, pulsing with a slow, deliberate heartbeat.

Lines of corrupted code crawled across the screen, like veins branching through rot.

An ancient ledger or the ghost of it unspooled into the dark.

Somewhere beyond the city, far beyond what Jonah Raines could have fought, a signal crossed an invisible threshold. A new archive began compiling itself from the ruins: names, debts, betrayals rewritten not in ink, but in silicon and ash.

And far away, where no badge could reach and no warrant could break the locks, something... watched. Waiting. Smiling.

The system had learned.

The ledger was just the beginning.

Made in the USA
Monee, IL
05 May 2025